The Hound of Ulster

And now for the first time, the hosts of Connacht
and Leinster and the rest saw the man who had
played wolf-pack unseen on their flanks, the Hound
of Ulster, and saw him in the full terror of his battle
frenzy, the Hero light blazing upon his brow and the
jet of black blood shooting skyward to make that
murk like a rushing storm-cloud that hung above his
head. And indeed now it was not only with weapons
that he killed, for at the very sight of him rushing towards them behind his flying team, it is told how
once a whole company of Maeve's warriors fell dead
from sheer horror at the aspect of him.

THE
HOUND
OF ULSTER

RETOLD BY
ROSEMARY SUTCLIFF

WITH DRAWINGS BY
VICTOR AMBRUS

RED FOX

For Juliet
With the Author's love, and her
apologies for a story from the
wrong side of the Border

A Red Fox Book
Published by Random Century Children's Books
20 Vauxhall Bridge Road, London SW1V 2SA

A division of the Random Century Group

London Melbourne Sydney Auckland
Johannesburg and agencies throughout the world

First published by The Bodley Head Ltd 1963

Text © Rosemary Sutcliff 1963
Illustrations © The Bodley Head 1963

Red Fox edition 1992

Printed and bound in Great Britain by
Cox & Wyman Ltd, Reading, Berkshire

ISBN 0 09 997260 3

Contents

Author's Note

YOU can learn a lot about a people from their stories, because their stories show the way they think and feel and look at things. The Cuchulain Saga belongs to the Celts, the people of Ireland and Wales and the Highlands of Scotland, just as the story of Beowulf belongs to the Anglo-Saxons; that is very broadly speaking, to the English, and the Scottish Lowlanders. And neither Celt nor Saxon could have bred the other one's story, for they belong to two quite different ways of thinking.

However wild the happenings in the Saxon story, its feet remain firmly on the ground; and Beowulf and his companions are recognisably human beings grown to hero-size. But the Celtic tale leaps off into a world completely of the imagination, and the Red Branch Heroes have the blood of the Gods and the Fairy Kind (almost the same thing in Irish legend) running fiery in their veins. It is worth noticing this difference when reading either story, and remembering that in the main the people of Cuchulain and the people of Beowulf separately or mixed together are the stock that we in Britain are sprung from.

For the rest: I have used the modern names for most places, including the five Provinces of Ireland in the time of the Red Branch Heroes, Ulster, Munster, Connacht, Leinster and Tara, the High King's territory. And I have spelled the names of people in the 'Englished' way, Laery the Triumphant, for instance, instead of Laegaire Buadach.

'Geise' is a kind of magical bond or prohibition, very much like 'taboo'. I might have said that it was taboo to Cuchulain to

7

eat the flesh of a dog, or for Fergus Mac Roy to refuse an invitation to a feast; but it seemed better to keep the Irish word, even if it needed explaining. The important thing to remember about anybody's geise is that it *could not be broken*.

ROSEMARY SUTCLIFF

1. Dectera's Gift

THIS is the story of Cuchulain, the Champion of Ulster, the greatest of all the Heroes of the Red Branch. Listen, now.

In the great days long past, there was a King of Ulster whose name was Ross the Red, and Maga his Queen was a woman of the Sidhe, the Lordly Ones, whose home is in Tir-Nan-Og, the Land of Youth. And Fiachtna the Giant was their son, and Fiachtna's son was Conor Mac Nessa, and both of them after Ross were to be Kings of Ulster in their turn. But the time came when Maga was no longer content with Ross the Red, and since no one can hold the Lordly People against their will, they parted, and she became the wife of Cathbad, who, though he had not then a grey hair in his beard, was the wisest of all the Druids in the land. And Ross the Red took a second wife, and the name of that one was Roy—a mortal maiden, this time, for he had had his fill of the Lordly Kind—and the son she bore him was Fergus Mac Roy.

And Cathbad and Maga had three daughters, Dectera, Elva and Finchoom. And Finchoom's son was Conall of the Victories; and Elva's three sons by her husband Usna were Naisi, Ainle and Ardan, and Dectera's son was no other than Cuchulain himself.

And these are the names and kindreds that you must remember, for these, with their comrades and henchmen and the sons who came after them were the Heroes of the Red Branch, because they were all of them sprung from Ross the Red, or linked with him through his first Queen.

One Midsummer Eve when Conor had not long been King, Dectera his kinswoman went down with her fifty maidens to wash their clothes in the stream that ran below the Royal Dūn, at Emain Macha. And when the shadows grew long at evening, and still they had not come carrying their new-washed linen back up the hill, search was made for them beside the ford and under the ancient hazel trees. But not so much as a golden hair of them was to be found.

For many days Conor and his warriors searched through the length and breadth of Ulster, and far south into Ireland beyond, but all to no avail. 'They have heard the music of the Silver Branch and gone into the Hollow Hills, into Tir-Nan-Og,' said Cathbad the Druid. 'Dectera has gone to her mother's kind, and taken the others with her like a flock of birds behind their leader.'

Three years went by, and it was as though Dectera and her maidens had never been; and then on another Midsummer's Eve, a flock of small bright birds descended on the barley fields about Emain Macha and the little stone-walled plots where the half wild fruit trees grew, and began to destroy the ripening fruit. Word of this was brought to Conor Mac Nessa and it seemed to him that there was sport to be had, as well as the

saving of the crops. And so with a band of his household
warriors—with Fergus Mac Roy and young Laery the Triumphant and Bricrieu of the Bitter Tongue and others—he took
his pouch filled with sling stones, and set out. But try as they
would, they could not hit one of the small bright birds among
the apple boughs, and the birds for their part only flew a little
way and began to feed again. And when the warriors followed
them with fresh pebbles in their slings, they fluttered a little
farther—and the fluttering of them was like laughter—and so
drew the hunters on and on, until at dusk when they could
no longer see to sling the polished stones, the King and his
companions found themselves near to the fairy mound at
Brugh-Na-Boyna.

'It is too far to be going back to Emain Macha tonight,' said
Conor. 'It is past cowstalling time, and they will have closed
the gates and set free the ban dogs and we shall rouse the
whole Dūn and bring the women squealing round our ears.
We can make a fire and 'twill not harm us to sleep one night
fasting.' And so they made a fire of dry thorn branches and
lay down about it, wrapped in their cloaks with their feet to
the warmth, while one of their number sat up to keep the blaze
going, though indeed 'twas little there was to fear from the
wolves at Midsummer.

But Fergus Mac Roy was restless and could not sleep, so
that at last he said to himself, 'Ach, the moonlight is in my
feet that I cannot be still,' and he drew his legs under him and
went off along the banks of the river towards the fairy mound.
As he drew towards it, he saw that a little mist lay low about
the hillock, snail-silver in the light of the full summer moon;
and then it seemed to him that the mist flowered from silver
into gold, and that the light came no longer from the moon
but from within the mist itself, as though there were a hundred

torches blazing at the heart of it. And as he came to a halt, thinking maybe the thing was best not meddled with, a great burst of light opened upon him, and he saw that the gates of the fairy hill stood wide. Indeed it was no hill at all, but a King's hall greater and more glorious even than the Hall of the High Kings of Ireland at Tara itself; and he moved towards it as though his feet were drawn by the suck of a tide. There were half-seen shapes about him, and half-heard music in his ears more sweet than any harping in any King's hall of the world of men; and on the shining threshold a man stepped out to meet him, golden and fiercely beautiful, so that it seemed the light shone from himself and not from any torches at all, as one would not need torches with the sun blazing in a clear sky. And Fergus knew that even among the Lordly People only one could shine with such a flame, and that was Lugh of the Long Spear, the Sun Lord himself; and he shielded his eyes under his arm. But when he looked at the woman who had come also to stand in the gateway, his eyes grew cool again, for she was like the shadow behind the sun, as graceful and fine-drawn as the shadow of a wild cherry tree.

And looking at her, Fergus saw that she was the lost Princess Dectera.

'You are welcome, Fergus Mac Roy,' said Lugh the Sun Lord, 'most gladly welcome, tonight of all the nights there are.'

And Dectera said to him 'You are welcome as the rain in a dry summer on the orchards of Emain Macha, for my heart has looked of late for one of my own kin to come to me.'

'Not only I, but Conor himself and others of the Red Branch are close at hand, for a flock of birds led us on this way until we were too far from Emain Macha to return this night, and so we made a fire to sleep by, and there they sleep in their cloaks.

Give me leave now to go back and rouse them and bring them here, for they will weep for gladness to see Dectera again.'

Dectera smiled as though at a secret when he spoke of the birds that had led them. But she shook her head. 'You have seen me and you know that it is well with me and I am happy. Go back to the camp now, and sleep with the rest.'

And then it seemed to Fergus that the mist returned, and he found that he was running back towards the camp. He saw the gleam of the watch fire and ran towards it, between the sleeping warriors who startled awake at his coming, until he was beside Conor the King, who had risen to his elbow, flinging back the cloak from his dark head. 'Is there a wolfpack on your heels then, my Uncle?' he demanded, dashing the sleep from his eyes.

And dropping beside him, Fergus told his story, and he was gasping for breath, for he had been running hard. Before all was told, the young King was on his feet, and the rest of the warriors pressing about him, and he chose out several of the men and bade them go swiftly, swiftly to the fairy hill, and bring Dectera back to him with all honour.

And when the warriors were gone, running silently as they would be on the hunting trail, the rest cast more thorn branches on the fire and sat down on their haunches to wait. In a while and a while the warriors returned, but Dectera was not with them. 'Ach, you need not tell it. There was nothing there but the hillock in the moonlight, and it with a wisp of ground-mist about its loins,' Fergus said disgustedly, pulling up tufts of grass and throwing them in the river.

'All was as you saw it,' said Laery the Triumphant, and then to the King he said, 'My Lord, we have seen the Lady Dectera, and Himself who is with her. But she bade us to say to you that she is sick, and beg you to forgive her and wait a while;

and she bade us say that when the sickness passes from her, she will come, and bring with her a gift for Ulster.'

Conor's dark brows drew together, for he was not a patient man, but there was no other thing to be done. And so they waited, gathered about the fire, and from waiting they fell at last, every one of them, into sleep, as though the harp of the Dagda had laid its spell on them.

In the first green light of dawn, with the ringed plover calling, the warriors awoke, and stared with startled eyes at the thing they found in the midst of them. For there, wrapped in a piece of golden silk within a dappled fawn skin, and mewing for all the world like the ringed plover, lay a new-born man child!

The Princess Dectera had come and gone again, leaving behind her her promised gift for Ulster.

Fergus Mac Roy carried the babe in the crook of his shield arm back to Emain Macha, and they gave him to Dectera's youngest sister Finchoom, who had a child of her own a few months old. And Finchoom nursed the two together. They called him Setenta on his naming-day, and the Plain of Murthemney that runs from Dūn Dealgan southward into Meath was given to him for his inheritance. But it was little enough that Setenta cared for that, sprawling with Conall and the hound puppies about the threshold of the King's Hall.

When they were seven summers old, and besides being cousins and foster brothers, were grown to be the closest and staunchest of friends, Setenta and Conall went to the Boys' House, where the sons of the princes and chieftains of Ulster learned the lessons that would make them warriors when the time came. And there, Setenta found the second of the three friends who were to be dearest to him through all his life. And this was Laeg, son of a Leinster noble killed in a cattle raid, who had been set in Conor's household for a hostage when he was yet too young to know the meaning of what had befallen him, and had long since forgotten that he was anything but Ulster-born among his own kind. He was a year older than Setenta, a tall boy, red-haired, and freckled as a foxglove; and such a way with horses he had that even at eight years old he had but to whisper in the ear of an angry stallion for the beast to grow gentle as a filly foal.

One day when Setenta was nearing the end of his time in the Boys' House, King Conor and his nobles were bidden to a great feast at the Dūn of a certain Cullen who was the greatest swordsmith in all Ulster, and young Setenta was to go with them—for was it not time, said Conor, that the boy learned the ways of courtesy as well as the ways of war? But he forgot the time of day and when the hour came for setting out, he was in the middle of a game of hurley with his companions, and standing, hurley stick in hand at the King's chariot wheel, he explained, 'If I come now, we shall lose the game.'

Conor smiled in the black of his beard. He was a stern man easily moved to anger, but he was fond of this small dark fighting cock of a cousin and allowed him freedoms that he would not have allowed to any other of the Boys' Band. 'What's to be done, then?'

'Let my Lord the King ride on,' Setenta said, 'and when the game is over and we have won, I will follow.'

So the King laughed and rode on with his nobles, and Setenta went back to his companions.

At dusk, Conor and his warriors reached the Rath of Cullen, and the master smith made them warmly and richly welcome, and brought them into his house-place and feasted them on fresh boar meat and badger's flesh roasted with wild honey, and fine imported Greek wine in splendid bronze and silver cups of his own forging. Meanwhile his people, not knowing of Setenta's coming, or else forgetting about it, dragged the night-time barricade of thorn bushes into the gateway, and let loose Cullen's huge hound, who guarded his master's house so well and mightily that Cullen, who loved him, was wont to boast that with his dog loose in the forecourt he feared nothing less than the attack of a full war host.

In the midst of the feasting, with the harp music leaping to the firelit rafters, there rose an appalling uproar in the night outside, a baying and yelling that brought every man to his feet and snatching up his weapons. 'Here is your war host, by the sound of it!' Conor said, and ran for the doorway, the lord of the house beside him and the warriors pounding at their heels. Men with torches were running towards the outer gates, where the yelling and snarling had sunk suddenly and horribly silent. And in the ragged glare of the torches, Conor and his warriors saw that the gate pillar was splashed with blood, and the thorn bushes had been thrust aside from the gateway, and in the opening, with the moon-watered darkness of the night behind him, stood Setenta, breathing like a runner after a race, and looking down at the body of the great speckled wolfhound that lay dead at his feet.

'What has happened here?' Conor demanded.

The boy looked up at their coming, and said, 'He would have killed me, so I killed him.'

And Cullen said harshly, 'How was it done?'

And Setenta looked at his hands as though he were seeing them for the first time. 'I caught him by the throat as he sprang at me, and dashed his life out against the gate pillar.'

'Ach now, that was a deed that few among full-grown

warriors could perform.' Conor beat his fist against his thigh
in approval, and there was a roar of praise and laughter from
the men about him.

Only Cullen the Swordsmith stood silent, staring down at
the body of the great hound; and all the lines on his face were

cut heavy with grief as with one of his own sword blades. And as they looked at him, a silence fell on the rest, so that they heard the night wind and the spluttering of the torches. Setenta broke the stillness, looking slowly up into the man's face. 'Give me a whelp of the same breed, Cullen the Swordsmith, and I will train him to be all to you that this one was. And meanwhile, let you lend me a shield and a spear, and I will be your guard-dog and keep your house as well as ever hound could do.'

Cullen shook his head, and set a hand kindly enough on the boy's thin shoulder. 'It is a fine offer, but I can still train my own hounds. Go you back to your own training, for it is in my heart that when the time comes, you will be the guard-hound of all Ulster.'

'And meanwhile,' said Fergus Mac Roy proudly, for he had never forgotten that it was himself had carried Setenta back to Emain Macha in the crook of his shield arm on the day that he was born, 'let us call him Cuchulain, the Hound of Cullen, in remembrance of his first battle and the offer he made afterwards!'

And so they caught the boy up and carried him into the fire-lit hall, shouting his new name after him: 'Cuchulain! Cuchulain!'

And Cuchulain he remained, until the day that he went beyond the sunset.

2. A Day for Taking Valour

A SHORT while after the slaying of Cullen's hound, the time came for first Laeg and then Conall to Take Valour, which is to say, to take the weapons of manhood upon them, and bid farewell to the Boys' House. And Cuchulain was left behind to serve out the last months of his training.

But 'twas few enough Cuchulain served of those remaining months, for one soft autumn day with the colours of the world all rich and dark as though the bloom of bilberries were on them, he came up from spear practice, and passed close by the thicket of ancient hazels that dropped their nuts into the water above the ford of the stream. And under the hazel trees, Cathbad sat with some of the Boys' Band about him, propounding to them the laws of their people—for it was his task to teach them such things, together with star wisdom and the art of cutting the Ogham word signs on willow rods. The lesson was over, but as Cuchulain came splashing through the ford, there was laughter and a dappling of eager voices, for the boys, who were all of them near their time for becoming men, were trying to coax him into foretelling to them what days would be most fortunate for Taking Valour, for Cathbad was wise in other things than law and writing.

'I am tired. I have told enough,' Cathbad said.

'Of law, yes,' the others chorused, 'but this is another thing.' And one of them, Cormac Coilinglass, the second son of the King, leaned forward with his arms across his knees and grinned at him. 'If you give us a day under good stars for our starting out, shall we not be like to do you the more credit among men, master dear?'

Cathbad smiled into his long beard that was still streaked with gold, though the hair of his head was white as a swan's wing; but under his white brows was a frown. 'Children, children you are, seeking to make the old man prance for you like a juggler with apples and silver cups. This much I will do, and no more. I will tell you what fortune lies upon this day, waiting for any boy who Takes Valour on it,' and he smoothed a space on the bare earth before him, and shook red and white sand upon it from two horns at his girdle, and began with his long forefinger to trace in the sand the strange curved lines of divination, while Cuchulain his grandson checked and stood watching with his hand on the trunk of the nearest hazel tree. Cathbad was scarcely aware of him, as he stooped frowning over the patterns in the sand, for he never put forth the least part of his power without giving to it his whole self, as though the fate of all Ireland hung upon what he did. He drew more lines and studied them, frowning still, while the boys crowded closer, half of them breathing down his neck, then he brushed all smooth again, and looked up, slowly, pressing his hands across his eyes, as though he would brush away the things that he had seen. 'The boy who takes up the spear and shield of manhood on this day will become the greatest and most renowned of all the warriors of Ireland, men will follow at his call to the world's end, and his enemies will shudder at the thunder of his chariot wheels, and the harpers shall sing of him while green Ireland yet rises above the sea; but his flowering-time shall be brief as that of the white bell-bine, opening in the morning and drooping before night. For he shall not live to count one grey hair at his temples . . . I can see no more.'

Cuchulain turned away from the hazel thicket where the

nuts fell splashing into the water above the ford, and set himself to the steep heathery slope that was crowned by the turf and timber ramparts and the great gate of Emain Macha. Once within the gates, he went in search of Conor the King, and found him just back from the hunting, sitting at ease on the bench before the Great Hall, with his legs stretched out before him, and his favourite hounds at his knee.

Cuchulain went and stood before him, and Conor, who was at peace with the world after his day's hunting, looked up and said, 'Well now, and what will you be wanting, standing there so big and fierce, with your shadow darkening the sun?'

'My Lord the King, I come to claim the weapons of my manhood today. I have learned all that the Boys' House teaches, and now I would be a man among men.'

'Your time is not yet for close on another half year,' Conor said, startled.

'That I know, but there is nothing I shall gain by the longer waiting.'

Conor looked at him long under his brows, and shook his head, and indeed, slight and dark as Cuchulain was, and small for his age, he seemed very far as yet from being a man. 'Nothing save maybe a wind-puff of strength and a thumbnail or so of height.'

The boy flushed. 'Size is not all that makes a warrior, and as for strength—give me your hunting spears, my lord and kinsman.'

So Conor gave him the two great wolf spears that were still red like rust on the blade, and Cuchulain took them lightly and broke them across his knee as though they had been dry hazel sticks, and tossed the pieces aside. 'You must give me better spears than these,' he said, and it was as though deep within him a spark kindled and spread into a small fierce flame.

Conor beckoned his armour-bearer, and bade him bring war spears; but when they were brought, Cuchulain took them and whirled them above his head, and broke them almost as easily as he had done the wolf spears, and tossed the jagged pieces away. By now there was a crowd begun to gather, and Cuchulain stood in the midst of them, waiting for someone to bring him better weapons. They brought him more spears, and then swords, and each he treated as he had done the first, and flung contemptuously away. They brought chariots into the fore-court, and he smashed them as easily as he had smashed the spears, by stamping his feet through the interlaced floor straps and twisting the ash framing of the bow between his hands, until all the forecourt lay littered with wreckage as though a battle had been fought there. And at last Conor the King burst into a harsh roar of laughter and beat his hands upon his knees and shouted, 'Enough! In the name of the High Gods, enough, or we shall have not a spear nor a war chariot left whole in Emain Macha! Bring the boy my own weapons, my spears and sword that were forged for me by Goban himself, and harness him my own chariot, for 'tis in my mind that those are beyond even *his* breaking!'

So the King's armour-bearer brought out Conor's own angry battle spears headed with black iron and decked with collars of blue-green heron hackles, and his sword whose blade gave off fire at every blow like shooting stars on a frosty night; and the charioteer brought the King's chariot, with polished bronze collars to the wheel hubs and its wicker sides covered with red and white oxhides, and in the yoke of it the King's own speckled stallions that scorned any hand on their reins save that of Conor himself or his driver.

And Cuchulain took the spears and sword and strove to break them across his knee, and could not, though he strained

22

until the muscles stood out on his neck like knotted cords. 'These weapons I cannot break,' he said at last.

The King said, 'Keep them, then, since it seems that none others will serve you. See now if the chariot serves as well.'

So Cuchulain sprang up beside the charioteer, and the horses felt the stranger behind them and began to plunge and rear so that their own driver could do nothing with them and it seemed that they and not Cuchulain would crash their heels through the chariot floor. Then Cuchulain laughed, and the fire in him blazed up like the smoky flames of a wind-blown torch, and he caught the reins from the hands of the King's charioteer and fought the team as a man might fight with a hurricane. For a while the watchers could see little but the cloud of red dust, hear nothing but the trampling and neighing of the horses flinging their plunging circles about the forecourt, and the screech and thunder of the wracked chariot wheels—until at last Cuchulain reined the panting beasts back on their haunches close before the King, and the uproar fell away, and there above them in the unharmed chariot stood Cuchulain alone, for the charioteer had been flung clear in the struggle, looking down at them out of his dark face with a smile that was both triumphant and a little sad, as though he were saying to his own heart that all good things passed too soon, and the horses standing with heaving flanks in their traces, and the last red dust sinking, eddying down about the wheels.

'Assuredly you are a warrior, and there is no place for you in the Boys' House any more,' the King said.

And Cuchulain sprang down over the chariot bow to the horses' heads, and standing between them with his shoulders leaned against the yoke, he set an arm over the neck of each horse. 'Then if I am a warrior and have my war chariot, let the

23

King also give me a charioteer. No man can well fight his chariot and drive at the same time—not even Cuchulain.'

'Choose for yourself,' said Conor Mac Nessa. 'That is the right of every warrior.'

Cuchulain looked about him, and saw among the crowding warriors the red head and long freckled face of Laeg who had been with him in the Boys' House only a few months before. And he cared nothing for the fact that Laeg was older than himself and a noble's son and should be no man's charioteer, but called out 'Laeg! Hai! Laeg! There is none that can handle a horse like you. Let you come and drive for me, that we may be together when the war horns sound!'

And as for Laeg, he flushed like a girl under his freckles, and a light sprang into his eyes that made his whole face kindle, and he strode out from the rest to Cuchulain's side. 'Let any other man try for the place that is mine, Hound Cub!' and he bent his head before young Cuchulain as though he and not Conor Mac Nessa were the King.

By the time he was sixteen, Cuchulain had won for himself a place among the warriors that many an older one could not lay claim to. And dark and meagre and bird-boned as he was, women found him so good to look upon that wherever he went their eyes would follow him, and not only the eyes of the maidens, but those of other men's wives; until the warriors and chieftains of Ulster began to urge him to take a woman of his own from her father's hearth.

Cuchulain was willing enough, but though he liked all women, he found none that his heart called to, until one day, at the great three-yearly gathering at Tara, he saw among the maidens in the Hall of the High King Conary Mōr, one that seemed to him to stand out from among the rest like a wild swan among herring-gulls.

She was dark-haired almost as himself, and her skin white as mare's milk, and her eyes wide and proud and brilliant like the eyes of Fedelma, his favourite falcon. Her gown was green, dark as the leaves of the hill juniper, and balls of red gold hung at the ends of her long braids and swung a little as she moved among the warrior benches to keep the mead cups filled. Cuchulain touched the wrist of Fergus Mac Roy who sat next to him, and leaning as though to share the same cup, whispered, 'Who is she?'

Fergus saw where he was looking and said, 'That is Emer, the daughter of Forgall, Lord of Lusca.'

'She is very fair,' said Cuchulain.

'She is fair enough, but her thorn hedge is thick. Best leave her alone.'

'And what is the meaning of that riddle, old wolf?'

'Her father is called Forgall the Wily. He is a Druid of great power, and it is said that he looks none too fondly upon men who come seeking to take his daughters from his hearth.'

Cuchulain said nothing more, but he did not put the thing from his mind.

If Emer had been his for the plucking like a strand of honeysuckle beside the track, he would likely have thought no more of her, but as soon as he knew that she might be hard and even hazardous in the winning, he knew also that of all the women in Ireland she was the only one that could make life sweet for him. All that evening he watched her as she moved among the crowded benches, and when she was gone with the other maidens back to the women's quarters, he turned his watching to the dark proud Lord of Lusca instead, and wondered what way he could best win the daughter from her father's hearth.

He did not try to speak with Emer during the days at Tara, for it would be against all custom and courtesy to pay court to any maiden save in her own home. And if Emer had seen the young dark warrior, she gave no sign of it.

But when the Tara gathering was over for another three years, and all the chiefs and nobles and the kings had returned to their own places, he waited three days that he might not come upon her weary from the journey, and not having time yet to gather her own life about her again, and then he bade Laeg to make ready his chariot for a journey.

'Where do we drive?' Laeg said.

'To Dūn Forgall.' And Cuchulain and his charioteer looked at each other, and the laughter leapt between them, and the purpose under the laughter.

In Dūn Forgall, Emer sat under the apple trees within the curve of the turf rampart. Her maidens were with her, and together they were stitching at a rich hanging for her father's hall, working on the dark cloth strange beasts and birds whose spread wings and together-twined tails broke into looping sprays and leafed and blossomed like some fantastic thicket.

They heard the distant rumble of sound, and one of the girls looked up quickly, saying, 'Surely that was thunder?'

'Let us take the work and run indoors before it can be spoiled,' said another.

But the sky was clear overhead, and the sun cast the shadows of the apple branches across the coloured work. And Emer said, listening, 'Foolish! That is a chariot driven at racing speed. Your eyes are like a hawk's, Cleena. Do you climb up onto the rampart and tell us who comes.'

So Cleena ran her needle into the work, and sprang up and

climbed to the crest of the turf bank and stood looking out northward under her hand, while the distant thunder drew swiftly nearer and became the drum of horses' hooves and the clangour of the chariot behind them.

'Well and what do you see?' said Emer, laughing and impatient.

'I see a chariot indeed! Drawn by a pair of speckled horses such as the King of Ulster drives. Fierce and powerful, they are, tossing their heads and breathing fire from their jaws; and the sods that they throw up behind them are like swallows darting in their wake.'

'So much for the chariot and the team,' said Emer. 'Who drives?'

'I do not know—a tall man with curling red hair held by a fillet of bronze about his temples—with him——'

'Well?' said Emer, and she jabbed her needle into the embroidered stuff and ceased her stitching.

'A small man—a boy—no, a man, dark and sad but best to look upon of all the men of Ireland. He wears a crimson cloak clasped at the shoulder with a brooch of gold, and it flies from him like a flame in the wind of his going, and on his back is a crimson shield with a silver rim worked over with golden figures of beasts.'

'That sounds like Cuchulain of Ulster,' said Emer, 'for when I saw him in the High King's Hall at Tara, always until he laughed he looked as though he were listening to sad music in his heart . . . Come, we must go to welcome him, since my father is from home.'

And she gathered up her skirts and ran towards the hall, her maidens after her, with the many-coloured hanging gathered among them. And as they ran, they heard the thunder of hooves trample into stillness before the great gate, and the sound of running feet, men's voices and the barking of dogs.

When the chariot swept behind its team into the forecourt of the Dūn and Laeg circled wide about the grey weapon-stone in the midst of the place, where the warriors sharpened their blades in time of war, and brought the horses to a trampling halt, and Cuchulain sprang down with his shield clanging behind his shoulder, he found Emer and her maidens already gathered at the threshold of the hall. She came forward, bearing the brimming guest cup of age-darkened bronze and silver inlay, and held it to him, smiling. 'My father is from home, and in his stead, I bid you drink, stranger, and be welcome.'

Cuchulain took the cup, letting his fingers touch hers, and looked at her above the rim. 'Am I then so much a stranger? Will you tell me that you have never seen me before, Emer, daughter of Forgall the Wily?'

Emer flushed bright as a campion flower, but she did not take her eyes from his. 'It may be that I saw you at Tara, at the Great Gathering.'

'It may be that I saw you there also,' Cuchulain said, and they stood looking at each other, and though Emer had given him the guest cup, she did not bid him enter. And the maidens drew apart and watched them, while Laeg stood at the horses' heads and watched them too.

At last Cuchulain said, 'Will you not bid me enter?'

'My father is from home, and I do not know when he will be back.'

'It was not your father that I would see, this first time.'

'Who then?' she said, determined that he should speak it.

'Who but yourself, Emer?'

'Then still less should I bid you come in. For what would my father say and do at his coming home, if it were told to him

28

that his daughter had brought young warriors of another tribe into his hearth place, who came to speak with her when he was from home?'

'Only one warrior,' said Cuchulain, and his dark sad face flashed open into laughter. 'And he will be speaking with Forgall your father, when he returns.'

'So? And what would he say to my father, this one warrior?'

'That he wishes to take Emer the Fair to his own hearth,' Cuchulain said.

She felt for the carved doorpost behind her, and her breath caught in her throat. 'It might be that Emer the Fair has her own word to say as to that!'

And Cuchulain set his hands against the house-place wall on either side of her, so that he held the maiden captive without touching her. 'What word? What word, Emer?'

Emer was silent for a while, then she said, 'Listen, Cuchulain. My father will not lightly let me go from his hearth to another's, and he has champions among his household warriors who could break you across one knee as it was told to me that once you broke the war spears and the hunting spears of the Lord of Ulster. And if it were not so, my sister Fial is older than I, and it is her right to be first wed.'

'But I do not love your sister Fial,' Cuchulain said.

'How should you, when you have not yet seen her?'

'I have seen *you*,' Cuchulain said, and the voice of him soft and warm-under-the-soft as the breast feathers of a falcon.

And Emer said, 'That is talk for men, not for boys with their battles still unfought. And he that takes Emer's heart and Emer with it, must have a mighty sword-hand for the taking. Come back when you have slain your hundreds, and the harpers sing your deeds in the King's Hall, little Hound, and it may be that I will bid you to come in.'

So Cuchulain dropped his hands from the wall, setting her free, and turned and mounted into his chariot without another word.

3. The Bridge of Leaps

ALL the long road back to Emain Macha, and all the next day
and the day after, Cuchulain was silent, thinking how he could
best accomplish the great deeds that Emer demanded of him.

Now he had heard, one time, of a mighty woman-warrior
who lived in the Land of Shadows, which some say is in Skye,
and who could teach the arts of war better than any man to
those who came to learn from her. So on the third day he bade
farewell to Conall his foster brother, and to Laeg his
charioteer, saying, 'I am away over seas to find Skatha of the
Land of Shadows, and learn what she alone can teach me.'

Laeg would have come with him, but Cuchulain said, 'Can
you drive sea-swallows in the harness? I must go over seas to
find what I seek. Bide here until I come again, and keep my
horses swift and happy.'

And so he set out on his journey.

For a long while he wandered, seeking Skatha and the Land

of Shadows, and many a time he came near to disaster on the way. And when at last he stood on the edge of a vast bog that it seemed had no way round or over, he was near to admitting in despair that the end of his journey was come. But as he stood on the last hummock of firm land, mired to the thighs with the black sucking ooze—for he had not taken defeat easily —and looking out hopelessly across the distance beyond distance of rushes and fluttering silken tufts of bog grass and the treacherous mazes of sour green turf that lay over quaking ooze, and hearing nothing but the desolate soughing of the wind and the small greedy sucking noises that the bog made around his feet, he saw the figure of a young man coming towards him on feet so light that they did not stir one white tassel of the bog grass. A young man like a flame, like a ray of the sun when it pierces between storm clouds.

'May the sun shine on your path, Cuchulain,' said the young man, drawing near, as one friend greets another.

And at that time Cuchulain did not think it strange that the other should know his name. 'Indeed, if the sun were to dry a path through this bog for me, that would be a thing worth having,' he said wearily, 'for it seems to me that I have no path left, and I am weary and mired with seeking for one.'

'It is a great matter to you, that you cross this Plain of Ill Luck, to the other side?' said the stranger, smiling.

'It matters more to me than anything in all my life that has gone before.'

And suddenly Cuchulain saw that the young man was holding out to him a wheel that looked like an ordinary chariot wheel, but smaller—or maybe it was of no especial size at all. 'Then roll this before you as you go,' said the young man, 'and follow without fear.'

And then it was as though the sun was in Cuchulain's eyes,

dazzling him so that he blinked and as he blinked it was as though the sun went behind a cloud, and he was standing alone on the edge of the great bog, holding the strange wheel in his hand as though it had been a war shield.

At once he set the wheel rolling straight ahead over the bog, and strode out boldly after it. And the wheel rolled on, suddenly blazing with light that shot like the sun's rays from its rim, and as it went the heat of it made a firm path across the quagmire, and Cuchulain followed safely and dry shod, until he came to the farther side, and the wheel disappeared just as the stranger had done. And never until that moment did Cuchulain think to wonder who the man might be.

There were other adventures yet before him, other hazards and mischances and times when it seemed that his search could go no farther, but never again was he near to despair. And so at last he came to a broad valley dipping to the sea cliffs, and a broad sea inlet running far back into the throat of it, and in the midst of the inlet an island thrust up, set with plots and tatters of green grass among the black fangs of the rocks upon which the spray beat with every in-sweep of the waves. On the highest point of the island, worn like a diadem on its brow, were the three-fold grey stone ramparts of a mighty Dūn, and Cuchulain saw the smoke of cooking-fires and the bronze blink of weapons in the sun. And in the sheltered cliff-top hollow just before him, was a cluster of turf-roofed bothies and a horse corral; and he saw chariots upended against the house-place walls, and rough straw spear targets were set up, and several fine hunting dogs lay sleeping or scratching themselves in the sun; and on the level green space before the huts, boys and young men were playing hurley.

Cuchulain walked towards them, and as they saw him coming, the game broke up, and a tall boy with silver-fair hair hanging about his brown neck, who seemed to be something of a leader among them, came to meet him, the hurley stick still in his hand, and the others crowding at his heels.

'Welcome, stranger. Do you come to join us?'

'That depends,' Cuchulain said. 'What is this place?'

Some of the younger boys grinned and nudged each other at his not knowing, but the leader among them said courteously enough, pointing with the hurley stick, 'Yonder is the Dūn of Skatha the woman-warrior, and here on this side of the gulf we who have come to learn the arts of war from her have our lodging.'

'Then I am come to join you,' said Cuchulain, with the great gladness that was on him. 'I am Cuchulain, kinsman to Conor Mac Nessa the King of Ulster, and I too would learn the arts of war from this woman-warrior.'

'That makes good hearing!' cried the pale-haired leader, 'for many of us here are from Ireland. Myself, I am Ferdia, son to Daman, and my land is Connacht. Come now and eat, and quench the dust of the journey, and tell us the news of home, and if Slieve Cruachan stands where it stood last year.'

So the game of hurley was forgotten and, rejoicing, they bore Cuchulain to the big central hut, where the slaves were preparing the evening meal.

When he had eaten and drunk with the rest, he went out again with Ferdia, and looked across the gulf to the Dūn on its jagged cliff-crag beyond, and saw again the blink of weapons in the evening light, and heard the distant neigh of a horse, and the notes of a harp on the far-most edge of hearing. 'How does one come to the gates of this woman-warrior?' he asked.

And Ferdia laughed and shook his head. 'Every morning Skatha comes to us. None of us have ever crossed the chasm.'

But by now, narrowing his eyes against the arrows of the

evening sun, Cuchulain had made out some kind of bridge across the gulf, and so he said, 'And why would that be? That if there is a bridge for the woman to cross over, you may not cross the other way?'

'That is called the Bridge of Leaps,' said Ferdia. 'Come and look at it.'

So they went together and stood before the bridge, and it was a single span of rock, its upper surface worn smooth and slippery as an oiled sword blade, and but little broader. And they looked down into the depth of the gulf, where far below the sea tides were swinging to and fro and boiling among the black rocks on which sprawled the shapes of great grey seals and white-fanged walrus.

'There are two feats which Skatha teaches last of all to the warriors of her training,' Ferdia said, 'and one is the thrust of the Gae Bolg, the Belly Spear that no armour may withstand, and the other is the Hero's Salmon Leap, which is the leap across the bridge. For if a man will step on the end of it, the middle bucks like a killer colt and flings him back, and if he leaps upon the centre, he is most like to miss his footing and plunge down to the rocks and the sea monsters.'

But Cuchulain was in no mood to wait until morning should bring Skatha out across her bridge, and he said, 'Yet give me an hour to rest after my journey, and it is in my mind that I can do it.'

'Don't be crowing too loudly before your spurs are grown,' Ferdia said. 'Besides, the sun will be down in an hour.'

'There will be a moon, later,' said Cuchulain.

And so the two walked back to the bothies, each busy with thoughts of his own.

Cuchulain wrapped himself in his cloak and lay down beside the fire in the central hut and slept for a while, the light ear-cocked sleep of the hunter. And the sun went down into the dark, and the moon climbed out of the dark. Then he woke and got up and stretched, feeling the weariness of the journey gone from his body, and walked out of the hut circle towards the Bridge of Leaps. And most of the others thronged after him, laughing and jesting, for he had made no secret of what he meant to do.

The gulf was a black gash in the moonlight, and the narrow bridge was slippery—shining as though a vast snail had crawled over and left its track of silver slime behind. And when he saw it straight before him, he flung off his cloak and began to run, swifter and swifter until on the very brink of the chasm he gathered himself and sprang for the centre of the bridge. He landed just short of it, and the bridge leapt upward, rearing like a killer colt, and flung him back among the young warriors who had come down to watch the game. Furious, he sprang to his feet and again ran for the bridge and sprang; and again the bridge reared up and tossed him contemptuously back. Yet again he sprang and yet again for the third time he was flung off into the midst of his companions. He was bruised and battered in body and spirit, and there was a roar of laughter from the young warriors, and Ferdia cried out as he struggled again to his feet. 'Best wait for Skatha in the morning, little whelp! Then if you cannot bide like the rest of us, maybe she will pick you up like a little lap dog and carry you across!'

Rage flared in Cuchulain's heart, and he shut his teeth and shouted back, 'Best wish me well in the next leap—even a lap dog can bite, and you shall know that, if I am flung back yet again among you.' And running forward for the fourth time, he summoned up all the strength that he knew was in him, and strength that he had not known was in him before, and leapt out over the abyss. The moonlight had turned red before his eyes, and great seas pounded in his head, but his foot was set firmly in the centre of the Bridge of Leaps, and with another bound he was across and racing up through the rocks and salt-crusted turf to the gates of the Dūn.

He beat upon the gates with his dagger. Watch dogs bayed and a voice quieted them. The great timber leaves were drawn back before him as though he were expected, and in the opening, with the light of her attendant warriors' torches making a blaze of her hair that was strong as the mane of a bay horse, stood a lean-faced woman in an old leather tunic and a kilt of saffron wool that reached barely to her knees, and the bronze ornaments and the white scars of a warrior on her arms. She stood leaning on a great spear and looking at him, with huge dogs crouching around her. 'And who are you that come to the Dūn of Skatha, when the fires are smoored for the night?' she said.

'I am Cuchulain, the Hound of Cullen, and I come to learn whatever you will teach me of the arts of war.'

'Rather, I should have said, watching you from the ramparts but now, that you were the Lord of All the Grasshoppers,' she said, and flung back her head and laughed at him with a snapping of white teeth that were big and square like a horse's. 'Go back now—you will find it easier this time—and do not make that leap again until I teach you the way of it; for the untaught man may chance to make it safely once, but not again; and a sad thing it would be to waste the best pupil who has come to me in years!'

So Cuchulain pressed his spear to his forehead in the way of a warrior saluting his chieftain, and swung on his heel and strode down once more to the Bridge of Leaps. And this time it was as broad as a buckler and as easy to cross as the ditch-causeway into Emain Macha.

The rest were still gathered on the other side, and he made at once for Ferdia, who stood out from his fellows by the great height of him and the fair hair in the moonlight, and already his hand was on the hilt of the hunting knife in his belt. 'It can be done, you see, Ferdia Son of Daman,' he said. 'And in Ulster we do not jibe at the newcomer in our midst. It seems that Connacht needs a lesson in courtesy.' And to the rest, 'Stand back and give us room!'

But Ferdia sat himself down on a rocky outcrop, and smiled up at him in the white moonlight, his knife untouched in his belt.

'Up!' Cuchulain said. 'Get up, Ferdia of Connacht! You are so big and strong, you cannot be afraid of a little lap dog, even though it has teeth!' He drew nearer, and stood over Ferdia with his knife in his hand, while the rest stood silent in their circle, watching.

And Ferdia, who had been sitting as still as the rock beneath him, came to life with the swiftness of a bowstring released, and dived straight for his knees.

Cuchulain was spent with his desperate leap, and off his guard. His feet whipped from under him and he went down with a thud that drove the wind from his body. And next instant Ferdia was lying on top of him with his long legs twisted round Cuchulain's, and his big hand pinioning Cuchulain's dagger wrist to the grass. And the circle of young warriors drew inward a little. Still crowing for breath, Cuchulain shut his teeth and struggled to get free; and then suddenly he felt an odd shaking in the body of his adversary, and knew that of all unlikely things, the big fair Connachtman was laughing. 'Lie still!' said the choking voice of Ferdia, 'Lie still, little black fighting-cock. My mother loves me and I am too young and beautiful to die.'

And in his surprise, Cuchulain lay still. 'Those who do not wish to die should take better care who they choose to jest with,' he said.

'I know, I know, but think before you slay me.' Ferdia whispered the last words with his mouth against Cuchulain's ear. 'Three times the bridge threw you back, and if I had not made you angry, would you have found that last extra feather-thrust of strength to make the leap, after all?'

And Cuchulain grew suddenly thoughtful, lying there in the cliff-top grasses, and let his fingers uncurl from the hilt of his knife; and then he began to laugh too. And in a little they got up and walked back towards the bothies, each with a hand on the other's shoulder, and heedless of the rest of Skatha's pupils who jostled and thrust behind them, demanding to know what the jest might be.

4. The Princess Aifa

In the months that followed, Cuchulain learned from the
woman Skatha all that she had to teach, save that she did not
yet deem him ready to learn the Hero's Salmon Leap, nor the
use of the Gae Bolg, the dreaded Belly Spear.

When Cuchulain had been half a year in the Land of
Shadows, there came war between Skatha and the Princess
Aifa, who, for all her youth, was almost as great a warrior as
Skatha herself and had many and many more chariots and
fighting men to follow her. For a long while past, Aifa had
cast eager eyes towards the rich cattle runs of Skatha under the
mountains, and begun to loose her young men in ever-growing
cattle raids across the border. And when word was brought in

to the Land of Shadows by a runaway slave that Aifa was gathering her war host, Skatha knew that her strongest chance lay in carrying the war into her enemy's country before the other chieftainess could be ready to receive her. And as soon as the harvest was got in, she gathered her own warriors and made ready her chariots. She did not call upon the younglings of the War School to follow her, but they caught up their weapons to come all the same, with Ferdia and Cuchulain at the head of them.

But Skatha was by no means sure of victory, knowing only that she and her people must fight or be enslaved, and though she seemed to accept all the young warriors of her War School, she determined that Cuchulain, who had no equal among them saving Ferdia Mac Daman and was not yet come to his full strength, and who, moreover, she had come to love better even than she loved her own two sons, should not be hazarded in such a desperate venture. And so on the morning of their setting out, she mixed certain sleepy herbs into the cup of wine that she sent him from her own before-dawn meal. And when, the meal eaten and the camp fires trampled out, the warriors rose to take their chariots, Cuchulain lay asleep with his head in the hollow of his shield.

And when Ferdia came striding through the camp to tell her that he could not rouse the Hound of Cullen, she said, 'Do not try. He will sleep for a day and a night and wake with no harm come to him.'

So Ferdia went back to the rest, and told them what Skatha had done, and they growled among themselves that it was a woman's trick, and were angry for Cuchulain's sake, but there was nothing to be done save take their places with the rest of the host who were already swinging their chariots out on the war trail.

But the drug that would have held most men sleeping for a day and a night, held Cuchulain for only an hour, and when he woke to find himself beside the black still-warm scar of a camp fire, he knew what Skatha had done, and he would have been angry for his own sake, save that there was no time to waste in anger. He snatched up his shield and his two great war spears, and set out in the wake of the rest, his buckler banging behind his shoulder at every step. For a long while he followed by the ruts of the chariot wheels, travelling at the swift untiring lope of a wolf in a hurry. He crossed the ford of the hill stream where they had made their midday halt, and before the shadows began to lengthen, saw far ahead of him the faint dust cloud rising behind their rearguard, and quickened his pace like a hunter when the quarry comes in sight.

And in a while and a while he was running straight up through the long dark wild-goose skein of men and horses and chariots, who called their greetings to him and cheered him as he ran, until he came at last to the side of Skatha's chariot, where she drove with the vanguard. 'Chieftainess, you do not mix your wine strong enough, for the man who drinks it will be sober again in an hour!'

And she looked down at him over the chariot rim, and sighed. 'I might have known that where there was fighting in the wind, Cuchulain could not be held back from it.'

At noon next day, the armies of Skatha and the Princess Aifa came together. And in a broad valley where the black rock ridges cropped through the heather they drew up the battle lines and grappled with each other, and the thunder-roll of meeting shields made the hills shake all around them. And all the rest of that day there was red slaughter on both sides, and Cuchulain and Ferdia fighting shoulder to shoulder with the two sons of Skatha, killed, among others, six of the best and bravest of the Princess's warriors, part of her inmost bodyguard.

Sunset came, and the two hosts drew apart to lick their wounds. And on both sides of the glen the watch fires were lit, and food and drink doled out to the tired warriors. And then, and not until then, Skatha swayed and sank to her knees beside the fire, and when Cuchulain ran to support her and put back the heavy dark folds of her cloak that made red stains on his hands, he saw that her sword arm was laid open to the bone.

Her sons and the other warriors came thronging round her. One brought wine in his warcap, and Eoghan the Druid, who was skilled in the tending of wounds, came hurrying with strips of linen and pungent-smelling wound salves, and knelt by her side, and taking the wine that she had barely tasted, began to cleanse the wound with it.

'Bind it tightly,' she said. 'There will be more fighting to-morrow, and I must lead my warriors even if I lash myself to my chariot bow.'

And the Druid said nothing, and the warriors looked at each other with a dark cloud spreading over their thoughts of the next day.

But there was to be no more fighting for the war host, that time.

For in the darkest hour of the night, those who were wakeful about the dying fires heard a challenge from one of the pickets, and even as they sprang up, snatching at their weapons, two of Skatha's men stepped into the leas of the firelight, and between them a man wearing the white swan's feather tuft in his war cap that marked him for one of Aifa's bodyguard, who carried no weapon but the green branch of a herald in his hand. 'Here is one who would speak with Skatha the Chieftainess,' said one of the picket warriors. Skatha had roused with the rest and was sitting upright on a pile of skins beside the fire, where she had been trying to sleep; her cloak drawn about her so that no man should see her wound. And when the herald was brought to her, he touched the green branch to his forehead, and stood waiting for her leave to speak.

'You bring me some word from the Princess Aifa?' she said.

'The Princess sends you, through my mouth, these words: "Skatha, chieftainess of many spears and my enemy, both our war hosts are weary and their wounds are deep. If we fight again today as we fought yesterday, and maybe the next day, and the next after that, what shall it avail us which triumphs in the end, when we are so weakened that any hungry chieftain may step into our land, and we lying up to lick our wounds? Therefore, let us fight the thing out in single combat, in the open between our war hosts an hour after sun-up, and the war hosts shall play no part in it save that men of mine and men of yours together shall fix the battle ground."'

When he had finished speaking, there was a long silence, and then Skatha said, 'I have listened to the words of the Princess Aifa, but I must have time to look into my heart and make sure whether they are good or bad. Therefore, do you go and drink a cup of mead beside the lower fire, and come back in the half of an hour, and you shall have my answer to carry back to the Princess.'

'The Princess Aifa likes not to be kept waiting,' the herald said. But Skatha pointed towards the fire with her left hand, and her face was bright with angry scorn. 'Nor does the Chieftainess Skatha like to be prodded along like a dawdling sow on the way to market!'

But when he was gone, she looked about her at her warriors, and said, 'What am I to do? What can I do? I cannot use my sword arm, and if the war host fights again, even though we gain the victory, it is as she says, and we may lose all beside.'

Then before anyone else could speak, Cuchulain said, 'Skatha, my master-in-arms, let me give proof now, whether you have taught me well.'

Skatha looked at him with pain-darkened eyes. 'If you mean what I think you mean, I tell you no. I do not need unbearded boys to fight my combats for me.'

'Will you fight your own, then, with a sword arm that you can scarcely lift from your side?' Cuchulain said.

And there was a blur of voices as the warriors came closer in, and man after man thrust forward, claiming his own right to take her place in combat against the Princess Aifa.

But Cuchulain said, 'Do not listen to them, Skatha; 'twas I spoke first, and to *me* is the right to take your place against this fighting princess.' And then leaning towards her as he half knelt at her side, he said, 'Skatha, you owe me that, for the trick with the winecup!'

And Skatha thought, and said at last, 'Surely, I owe you that. So be it, then, but do not cry to me from beyond the sunset!'

'Tell me one thing, then, if you can, and I will not,' Cuchulain said. 'What is it that Aifa loves most in all her heart?'

'What Aifa loves best in all her heart,' Skatha said, 'are her horses and her chariot and her charioteer.'

And Cuchulain laughed, and went to see his weapons.

And by and by the herald went back to his own chieftainess with Skatha's word. 'I, Skatha of the Land of Shadows, greet you the Princess Aifa, and sorrow it is to me that I cannot meet you sword to sword, for I am something hurt in the

45

sword arm. But in my place I send you Cuchulain of Ulster, to be my champion; therefore, let you choose a champion in your turn, or come yourself against the champion I send, as you would if it were I . . .'

An hour after sunrise Cuchulain dropped from Skatha's own chariot at the place of combat that had been chosen by the captains on both sides, and turned to look up at Ferdia who had come with him as his charioteer and weapon-holder, saying, 'Keep the horses well back.' Then he swung his shield round from his shoulder, and walked forward with his throw-spears ready in his hand to meet the shining figure that came towards him through the heather and bilberry scrub. The chosen place was a piece of level ground that ran out from the black-bloomed mountainside into clear view of both war hosts; and beyond it, suddenly the whole glen fell away into a deep gorge, and a honey-brown hill burn plunged downward with it, arched and white as a stallion's mane.

The enemy champion had left chariot and driver on the far side of the level place, and the rays of the rising sun made a rim of fire round chariot and charioteer and fidgeting team, with nothing beyond them but the darkness of the mountain slopes across the glen. But Cuchulain was watching the figure as it drew towards him, trying to guess at the mettle of the warrior he must meet. And as the figure drew nearer, he saw that it was Aifa herself had come out against him, just as he had hoped.

She too had her rim of sun-fire round her, and the hair that spilled from under her war cap seemed a yellow cloud, as it would be the pollen-cloud that shakes from a hazel tree in March when the wind blows by; and the plates of bronze that covered her war-tunic rang together as she moved, and for all its weight and the weight of the great round buckler and the two spears she carried, she walked as lightly as a red hind along the hillside.

Cuchulain heard the roar of the watching war hosts like a storm in his ears as he began to run, and the Princess Aifa also began to run, and they came together in the midst of the level place, and saluted each other with their spear tips. And the salute done, they fell to the fight, circling about each other, each seeking to get the sun at his own back and in the other's eyes, while the war hosts were silent, remembering what hung upon their spear points. First they drew off, and each threw their javelins, but each took the light throw-spears on their shields with no harm done; and then they closed in with the broad in-fighting spears, and when the spears were blunted and bent on their shields, they cast them aside as by common consent, and drew their swords. Long and long they fought, circling and crouching in the heather, trying on each other every thrust and parry and champion's trick that they knew, yet neither able to gain the advantage though both were bleeding from more wounds than one. And then at last Cuchulain caught his foot in a heather snarl, and in the instant that he wavered off the balance, Aifa leapt upon him like a wild beast, their swords rang together, and Cuchulain's sword that had been the battle-sword of Conor Mac Nessa himself flew into a hundred shining fragments.

Cuchulain sprang back, with the useless hilt still in his hand, and in the instant before she could spring after him, he shouted, glaring wildly past her, 'The horses! Name of Light! The horses! They're over the edge and the chariot with them!'

And as Aifa cried out and snatched one frantic glance

behind her, he flung his shield one way and the sword hilt the other and sprang. His arms were round her waist, crushing the breath out of her against the bronze scales of his own armour. With a scream of rage she flung aside her own sword that she could not use at so short a range, and he was just in time to grasp her wrist as she went for the dagger in her belt, and wrench it behind her. She fought like a mountain cat, not hitting man-wise, now that she was captive, but clawing at his face with her free hand, and struggling to get her head down to bite his neck where it rose from the band of his war tunic. And Cuchulain laughed and crushed her harder and harder against him until the breath was all driven from her and she could fight no more. And then he flung her across his shoulder, and turned back to his own chariot.

Ferdia brought it to meet him, laughing as he leaned back on the reins. 'What have you there?'

'A wild cat, and its claws are sharp!' Cuchulain scrambled in and the horses sprang away, wheeling and breaking into full gallop, back towards the camp of Skatha, while Aifa's own charioteer, swinging his team half-circle, came thundering after them, and the roaring of the war hosts rose even above the drumming of hooves and the clangour and screeching of the chariot wheels.

They reached the fringe of their own host, and the warriors closed in behind them to cut the pursuit, and in the clear space before the branch shelter that had been woven for Skatha Ferdia brought the team to a trampling halt, and Cuchulain sprang down with his captive still powerless across his shoulder, flung her on the ground, and next instant was kneeling over her with her own knife at her throat. In all the camp of the war host it seemed that no one moved, not a horse in the picket lines nor the youngest armour-bearer, nor Skatha herself, standing hollow-eyed in the entrance to her shelter and looking down at her foe.

The Princess Aifa looked up past Cuchulain into Skatha's face, and said, 'Chieftainess, if ever you loved the swiftness of a horse under you or the balance of a spear in your hand, grant me my life that I may know them again. It is one thing to die in battle, but this is another thing.'

'Ask that of Cuchulain of Ulster,' said Skatha. 'Your life is his, not mine.'

And so suddenly Cuchulain found her looking up into his face, and he saw for the first time that she was beautiful, with the beauty of a tempered sword blade or an arrow's flight that is dear to the heart of a fighting man. 'If my life is yours,' she said, 'be as open handed as you are strong and give it back to me. It is well that those who are renowned as warriors should be renowned as gift-bestowers also.'

'I will give you back your life,' said Cuchulain, 'if you will swear on the Great Stone of Tara that you will never again threaten war against the Chieftainess Skatha, nor come trampling across her borders to drive off her cattle and horse herds, but keep the peace between your lands and hers.'

'On the Great Stone of Tara, I swear,' Aifa said, with the dagger still at her throat.

And Cuchulain withdrew the dagger and sent it spinning towards the feet of Skatha the Chieftainess, where she still stood in the opening of her shelter. 'There is one thing more. We have dead men to be buried, and wounded among us too sick for the jolting of the chariots. Therefore, we make the Death Fires here for those that have gone beyond the sunset, and bide on in this place until our wounded may be moved; and that we may sleep easy in our minds at nights, you shall send home your warriors, but *you* shall remain here in our midst, until the time comes that we go home to our own hunting runs.'

'I understand,' said Aifa. 'Only let me go to the edge of my own camp to tell this thing to my warriors—you shall send men with me to be sure that I do not break faith—and I will bide as hostage for my war host while you remain in this glen.'

And so when the sun went down that night and they kindled the Death Fires, a second shelter woven of green branches stood not far from Skatha's; and the Princess Aifa slept there, on Cuchulain's crimson cloak that he had spread for her.

5. Cuchulain's First Foray

FOR many days Skatha's war host remained encamped on one side of the glen, while on the other the few who yet lived of Aifa's bodyguard remained also, after the rest of her war bands had departed. And for many days the Princess Aifa remained among her foes as a hostage. But to Cuchulain she was more than a hostage, and in those days while the bell-heather passed its glory and began to die, and the burn ran yellow with the first fallen birch leaves, he forgot Emer working at her embroidery under the apple trees of Dūn Forgall, and loved the Princess Aifa in her stead.

At last the time came when the sorest wounded might be moved, and they harnessed the horses and turned back towards

the borders of the Land of Shadows. And the Princess Aifa
went with them in the dust cloud behind the chariots, marching
with Cuchulain in the ranks of the Warrior School, while
always her own bodyguard kept faithful pace with them, a
spear-throw to one side. At noon they came to the stream
that was the border between the two lands, and there they
halted. And there with the eyes of the whole war host upon
them, Cuchulain and Aifa took hands and walked together a
little way downstream.

They halted in the shelter of a thicket of blackthorn that
would be fleeced with grey-white blossom in the springtime,
and Cuchulain pulled a gold ring from his finger and gave it to
Aifa. 'When running water is between us, we shall not meet
again,' he said, 'but if you should bear me a son, Aifa flower-
of-my-heart, send him to me in Ulster when the time comes
that his hand is big enough for that ring.'

And Aifa said, 'Have you any other bidding for me, Hound
of Ulster?' not as a warrior speaks, and not as a chieftain, but
as a woman accepting the thing that must be.

'Let you call him Connla,' Cuchulain replied. 'And when
the time comes that you send him to me, put him under this
geise, that he shall not tell his name to any who ask it on his
way; that he shall not turn out of his way for any man's bidding; that he shall never refuse a combat, for the sake of the
combat that was between you and me.'

'I will remember,' the Princess Aifa said, and she set her
hands for an instant on either side of his face, over the bronze
cheek-flanges of his war-cap, and looked deep into his eyes.
'Do you remember also, when that time comes!'

And she dropped her hands and turned and walked away
with never a backward glance, towards where her waiting bodyguard stood leaning on their spears. And Cuchulain rounded

on his heel and strode off to rejoin the war host of Skatha
that was already splashing through the ford.

The year and a day were almost up, and Cuchulain had
mastered all the skills and all the warrior feats that Skatha had
it in her power to teach him, even to the Hero's Salmon Leap
and the manner of using the Gae Bolg, which when it struck
into the belly of any enemy, filled all his body with its deadly
barbs. And for a parting gift she had given him a sword of her
own in place of the sword he lost in fighting the Princess Aifa
and the Gae Bolg itself which she had never thought any
other champion worthy of, not even Ferdia Mac Daman.

And so it was time for Cuchulain to take leave of the Land
of Shadows, and his fellows of the Warrior School. Time that
he must be taking his leave of Ferdia, who had been his fiercest
rival in all that time, and was nearer to him even than Laeg or
Conall his foster brother. And until it was upon him, he had
not known how sore that leave-taking would be.

'Why could you not be a man of Connacht?' Ferdia demanded with his heavy arm across Cuchulain's shoulders.

'And why could not *you* be a man of Ulster?'

They swore the Blood Brotherhood together on the last
night of all, and they swore to keep faith each with the other
so long as the life was in them. And they went their separate
ways, and little they knew how they should meet again.

So Cuchulain came back to Ulster, to Emain Macha once
more—and found Conall his foster brother lying beside the
fire in the Red Branch Hall, nursing a score of half-healed
wounds and a sword arm all but hacked from his body, and

heard from him how Conary Mōr the High King of Ireland was dead. How he and almost all his bodyguard had been slain at the great Inn of Da Derga, where he had been passing the night, slain by pirates out of Britain, and among them his own foster brothers that he had outlawed one time for robbery and cattle rieving.

'And what would you be doing among the High King's bodyguard?' Cuchulain asked.

And Conall shrugged. 'I had a little falling-out with Celthair Mac Uthica. Only a little falling-out, but King Conor bade me go and offer my services to Conory Mōr while Ulster cooled behind me.'

'And it seems your services were greatly worth the having! With the Inn burned down and the High King dead, how does it happen that you are here by the Red Branch fire, alive though somewhat scathed?'

'Ask the same question of two others of his guard. When the King was dead we three that were left fought our way out and came away,' Conall said, beginning to be angry.

Cuchulain was angry then, because he had not been at Da Derga's Inn. 'By the light of the sun, if I had been with the High King, they would not have slain him so easily!'

'There were some among us who did not lie down for them to swarm across our necks,' said Conall between his teeth, nursing his arm to ease the ache of it. 'A few blows we struck against the pirates, even though we had not the Hound of Ulster in our midst.'

But Cuchulain flung from the Hall, nursing his anger for the blaze of it within him that warmed the place still cold for the parting from Ferdia.

Yet when the anger sank at last, and he had made his peace with Conall, the soreness and the cold was in his heart again.

Then old wise Fergus Mac Roy saw that there was some grief in him, and knowing the best cure for such as Cuchulain, said to him on the third day after his return, 'Now it may be that you are the best fighting man in all Ulster, yet still you have to prove it. Would you think well of a foray along the marches of Connacht?' For between Connacht and Ulster there was always a fitful surf of skirmishes and cattle-raiding along the borders.

And Cuchulain said, 'Surely that is as good a way as any other to pass the autumn days.' And he laughed, and bade Laeg to yoke his horses and make ready the chariot, saying, 'We are away to burn off Connacht's gorse for them. They will be grateful to us!' and so set out on his foray.

'To the white cairn on Slieve Mourne, king of all the mountains of Ulster. From that eagle's eyrie a man can see far.'

And when they came there, he bade Laeg to pull up the horses, and turning about in the chariot he stood looking out over the hills and glens and the wide bogs and the ruffled lakes of Ulster, with the last flame of autumn on the bracken, and the heather black now as storm clouds upon the mountains, and the white gleam of the King's Dūn at Emain Macha, and the rolling country of Murthemney south and westward, with Slieve Cuillen and Slieve Fuad standing like warrior brothers to hold the Gap of the North that was the chief way from Ireland into Ulster. 'There I will build my own hall within the ring-ramparts of my own Dūn when I am Champion of all Ireland and have Emer to sit beside my hearth,' he said.

And then he turned full southward and looked out beyond, over the wide green plains of Bregia. 'Tell me the names of all the places that we can see.'

And Laeg pointed out to him Tara that was empty now of

the High Kings, and Teltin, and Brugh-Na-Boyna, and the great Dūn of the Sons of Nechtan.

'Nechtan,' Cuchulain said when he heard the name. 'Are they the Sons of Nechtan of whom it is said that among them they have slain more Ulster men than are now living on the earth?'

'They are so,' said Laeg.

'Then to visit the Sons of Nechtan we will go.'

Laeg looked at him, frowning his sandy brows. 'Do not play too rashly with this fire for the furze of Connacht. We are but two, and the Sons of Nechtan are many.'

'Nevertheless, I have a mind to visit them,' Cuchulain said, playing a little with the great war spear in his hand.

And so they drove with the swiftness of a scudding storm down through Murthemney and into Bregia, and it would have been three days' journey to any horses save those of Cuchulain's, with any charioteer save Laeg.

Now before the Dūn of the Sons of Nechtan was a wide green meadow on which the young men were wont to race their chariots and to practise the arts of war. And in the midst of the meadow stood a tall pillar stone worn smooth by the multitude of weapons that had been sharpened on it, and about the shaft of the stone was a bronze collar on which showed the word-signs of the Ogham script. And when Cuchulain had dismounted from the chariot and gone closer, he found that it set upon any stranger who should read it the geise that he should not depart again without meeting in single combat one of the seven brothers who were the lords of the Dūn.

Then he laughed. 'Surely there is no need of this stone and its message, for it bids me to do the very thing that brought me here!' and laughing still, he flung his arms round the great

56

stone and began to wrestle with it as though it were a living thing, heaving it to and fro until it came at last clear out of the earth into his arms. And then he flung it into the river that ran close below the Dūn.

Laeg, who had sprung down to stand at the horses' heads, cried out to him, 'You fool, Cuchulain! To go seeking adventure is one thing, but to go with both hands open, begging for a violent death, is another; and now you will surely find what you seek!'

The words were scarce out of his mouth before Foill the eldest son of Nechtan came striding down from the gate, just as he was, in a ram skin buckled with gold about his waist and no weapon in his hand. 'That was discourteously done!' he said. 'For what reason do you throw the pillar stone of my house into the river?'

'For a challenge, according to the words upon the collar.'

'All that is needful is to strike with the spear blade upon the stone,' Foill said with contempt. 'But I do not slay boys, even boys with the strength and foolishness to overthrow my pillar stone!'

'No, I know that you kill men—all the men of Ulster whose backs are to your spear! Now go and fetch out your weapons, for *I* slay neither drivers nor messengers nor unarmed men!'

Then Foill seemed to grow taller, and the brown hairs at his beard curled upward as though each hair had an angry life of its own. 'For that insult I will indeed fetch out my weapons,' he said deep in his throat as the snarl of a wolf, and turned and strode back towards the gates of his Dūn.

'Now what is to be done?' Laeg growled when he was gone. 'Did your nurse never tell you when she danced you on her knee, that Foill Son of Nechtan is proofed by magic spells against the edge or point of any blade? Not Lugh's bright spear itself can pierce his hide.'

'But this may,' Cuchulain said, and he brought from his breast his old supple sling, and set into its pouch a sling ball of iron mixed with silver; and he waited. And when Foill came striding back with his shield up and his war gear clanging on him, Cuchulain let fly at him with a shout like a boy letting fly at a marsh bird, and the sling ball struck him on the forehead and drove through war cap and bone into his brain, so that he leapt up into the air and fell face forward with no sound save the clangour of his armour.

Then Cuchulain sprang forward, drawing his sword, and with one mighty stroke shored through the strong neck of Foill Mac Nechtan, and pulling off the helmet, took up the head and knotted it by the long hair to his chariot rim.

Scarcely had he done so, when the second son of Nechtan, having seen from the ramparts the ill fate of his brother, came running, sword in hand; and him Cuchulain fought and killed with the sword, and knotted his head beside that of Foill to his chariot rim, while the horses stamped and snorted at the smell of blood; and so it went on until there were seven heads hanging for trophies at the rim of Cuchulain's chariot, and no more sons of Nechtan to take up the fight. Then Cuchulain cleaned his sword on the grass and bade Laeg to make fire from his fire-pot, and they pulled branches of heather and dead furze and dipped them in the flame and flung them blazing over the gate of the Dūn, and then galloped away, leaving the fortress roaring up like a great torch behind them.

All night they drove between the moon and the darkened heather, and at dawn a great flock of wild swans flew over, and Cuchulain brought down sixteen of them alive with his light sling stones and tied them to the chariot by long leashes of silk pulled from the hem of his tunic, so that they circled overhead as he drove; for by now, with the fighting and his triumph the battle frenzy was growing upon him, and he could perform feats of strength and skill that were beyond any man in his right nature. And when they saw in the distance a herd of deer, he bade Laeg to turn the horses after them and whip them to their fullest speed; then seeing that even such horses as his could not overtake them, he sprang down from the chariot and ran them down on foot, and took with his naked hands the two great stags who were the lords of the herd, and tied them with the spare picket ropes to the sides of the chariot as though they had been wheelers of a four-horse team. Then with Laeg lashing on the horses, they thundered on towards Emain Macha.

That evening at the Royal Dūn, a warrior of Conor Mac Nessa who had been on watch upon the ramparts went running to the King in such haste that he scarce remembered to touch spear to forehead in salute before he burst into the tale he had to tell. 'My Lord the King, there is a chariot rushing towards the Dūn, the like of which no man ever saw before, for wild swans circle above it and two stags are the wheelers of the team, and it is hung all round with the bleeding heads of enemies!'

Then Conor Mac Nessa snatched up his spear and hurried to the ramparts to see who it was that drove to Emain Macha in such strange manner. And looking out into the fiery light of sunset, he saw that the chariot-warrior was Cuchulain and that for the first time his full battle frenzy had come upon him. Now as the years went by this battle frenzy of Cuchulain's became a thing that all men knew and trembled at; and the way of it was this: from head to heel he quivered like a bullrush in a running stream, and the muscles of his neck stood out like the coils of a writhing serpent. One eye sank deep into his head, and the other thrust out, full of flames, and foam burst from his mouth like the fleece of a three-year-old ram and his heartbeats sounded like the roars of a lion as he rushes on his prey. A light blazed upon his forehead, and his hair grew tangled as the branches of a thorn bush. And from the crown of his head sprang a jet of dark blood that shot tree-high towards the sky and spread into a rolling murk that cast its shadow all about him.

And watching him now, as the wild team swept nearer, Conor the King knew that he was like a bull run wild and would slay all things in his path, whether friend or foe. He knew also that only one thing would hold him and that was the shock of shame; and he sent word swiftly to the maidens of Emain Macha to fling off their gowns and run and stand naked in his path when the gates were opened.

A score or more of the swiftest and most valiant did as he bade them, so that when Cuchulain crashed upon the gates of the Dūn like a thunderbolt, and they were flung back (since none might hold them against him) he saw the girls standing before him all across the way, naked as the day their mothers brought them into the world, with the sunset light flushing their bodies to the rose and gold of autumn honeysuckle. And shame pierced through his frenzy and reached him when nothing else could have done, that the girls of Emain Macha must do this because of him, and as Laeg fought the maddened team to a halt, and the wild swans beat in panic overhead, he bowed his head upon the chariot rim.

But still he quivered like an aspen tree, and the red light shone about his head, and Conor's warriors came running, a score of them together, and seizing him from the chariot, plunged him into a vat of cold well-water that had been made ready meanwhile.

Almost at once the water began to hiss and boil around him as though he were a red-hot sword for tempering, and the hoops of the great vat burst and the staves flew outwards, and they dragged Cuchulain from the wreckage and plunged him into a second vat and then into a third, until at last his battle-fury cooled, and they held in their midst only a slight, dark young man who seemed very weary.

And presently he went to his own place among the bothies of the Red Branch Warriors, and put on fresh clothes in place of those that were sodden and scorched and blood-fouled, and then went to supper in the King's Hall, just as though he had never set out to harry the Marches of Connacht.

6. Cuchulain's Wedding

Now that he had become a warrior indeed, Cuchulain knew that he could go to Emer whenever at all he chose, and that this time she would bid him to come in. But she had turned him away to please herself and now the girl should wait until it pleased him to come again. And so the days went by and he spent them hunting and hawking with his fellows, and did not go near Dūn Forgall at all. There was plenty of time for that, or so he thought.

And then one day, passing Fedelm the wife of Laery as she stood in the gateway of the Women's Courtyard watching a group of children at play, he would have stopped to pass the time of day with her; but she cast one look at him and turned away to leave him with the words of greeting half spoken.

Surprised and midway to laughter, he called after her, 'Now, Fedelm, do you shake me off like a dung beetle about your skirts?'

And she checked and looked back. 'Surely I may choose who I speak with and who I do not speak with?'

'I have never been one that you did not speak with before. What have you against me, Fedelm?'

Fedelm's eyes flashed upon him. 'I have this against you, that you forget too easily. Before you went to Skatha's War School you were hot as fire to take Emer from her father's hearth, and now you hunt and fly your hawks while the King of Munster comes courting her! It is in my heart to hope that her memory is as short as yours, for if not, it's crying out for you she'll be, since there's little mercy she'll get from Forgall her father, if her choice does not run with his! And you forget-ting her all the while.'

The laughter of Cuchulain went out as though she had struck him in the face. 'The King of Munster? Grief upon me! I did not know that was the way of it!'

'You might have known, if you had cared to listen. It is a thing that blows about on the wind, for any man to know.'

'However that may be, I did *not* know!' Cuchulain said. 'I did but mean that she should wait a little, in payment for the waiting she put upon me,' and he turned on his heel with no more said, and went striding off to the stables and chariot sheds, where the drivers were playing knucklebones in the autumn sunshine.

He shouted for Laeg his charioteer to yoke the horses with-out delay. 'We are done with hunting for a while, my King of Drivers! We are for the Dūn of Forgall the Wily, to bring home a bride.'

'It is not fitting that the groom should go without a groomsman at his back, to fetch the bride away,' said Laeg, leaving his game.

And laughter returned to Cuchulain and he called to Conall who was passing the stables, 'I am away to fetch my bride. Will you come with me for my groomsman?'

And Conall said, 'Surely, though it's little enough help I'll be, with the wounds scarce healed on me. I and who else?'

'Any who choose to come.'

'In that case you will be driving to Dūn Forgall with half the host of Ulster at your back.'

'Fergus Mac Roy, then,' Cuchulain said. 'Always he has been as a father to me, and it is right that he should come with me now. And Laery if he chooses, and the three sons of Usna. That should be enough, with the charioteers. Bid them all bring their weapons.'

And Cuchulain and Conall looked at each other, eye into kindling eye.

And so a little later when the shadows were shortening under the ramparts, Cuchulain set out at the head of six chariots, to fetch home Emer from her father's hearth though she were ten times promised to the King of Munster. And he and the Red Branch Warriors who followed him were clad all in the brilliant plaids of green and black and red and saffron, and the ornaments of gold and bronze that befitted a bridal party; and fluttering scarves were tied to the chariot rims; but each man's war cap hung among the coloured scarves, and under the gay mantles he wore his battle shirt, and he tossed up his weapons in his hand.

In the evening of another day they came thundering up through the faint frosty mist of late autumn to the great turf and timber walls of Dūn Forgall, and smelled the warm reek of the byres and the tang of wood-smoke hanging low in the evening air. It was still daylight, but already the gates were closed with the thorn barricades. And springing from his chariot Cuchulain beat his spear across his shield rim, calling for the people within to open up to him. A warrior stepped out of the mist on to the open rampart that flanked the gateway, and stood looking down at him, leaning on his spear.

'Who calls for entrance when the gates are closed?'

'Who closes the gates before cowstalling time?' Cuchulain called up, standing on widespread feet.

'Forgall the Wily closes the gates of his own Dūn in his own time. Who calls for entrance?'

'Cuchulain of Ulster, come to bring away his bride.'

Heads were showing all along the rampart now; the man's eyes widened, and he laughed and stepped back, and a few moments later, as Cuchulain still stood staring up at the crest of the timber facing, another figure appeared in his stead, the tall shape of Forgall the Wily, clad in the long dark robes that marked his rank among the Druid kind, with the sacred gold lunula on his breast but a naked sword in his hand.

'Go home again, Cuchulain of Ulster. It does not please me that any man should come shouting under the walls of Dūn Forgall for a bride.'

'Not even Lugaid of Munster?' Cuchulain shouted back.

Forgall's lips twisted in a smile. 'Would that be any concern of yours, my little hound puppy?'

For that moment, Cuchulain swallowed the insult. 'It is this concern of mine, that the thing has been settled between me and Emer this year and more. And as for this Munster kingling, save for a crown that sits unsure upon his head, what way would he have more to offer than myself? What better could you want for the maiden than the hearth of Cuchulain of the Red Branch of Ulster?'

'A hearth of my own choosing, and that not within Ulster's borders,' said Forgall.

'And you will not let her come out to me, though her own heart comes before her?'

'I will not.'

'Then,' shouted Cuchulain, 'it seems that I must come in to fetch her!' and he spoke over his shoulder to his comrades behind him; and then gathering himself together, he made the Hero's Salmon Leap up and clear over the strong ramparts of Dūn Forgall, and landed on his feet among the warriors inside. They rushed upon him from all quarters, and he dealt them three mighty sword blows, and at each blow eight men went down. Yet still others came crowding in on him, for Forgall kept many champions in his Dūn. And meanwhile, as he fought them, yelling his battle cry above the clash of weapons, those of Cuchulain's band still outside had brought out the fire-pot Laeg carried, and were flinging their kindled torches into the mass of dry thornwork that closed the gate, and behind him he heard the snap and crackle of it, and the roar as it went up in a sheet of flame. And through the fire and the rolling smoke, Laeg and the chariots, each driver crouching out along the yoke pole with his cloak flung over the horses' eyes, came crashing, and the warriors sprang down to Cuchulain's side even as the maddened teams clove into the mass of Forgall's men ahead of them. Now Forgall himself sprang at Cuchulain, big and deadly as a bull of the wild black mountain cattle, his eyes and his nostrils blazing red, but Cuchulain turned in one leap and took the blow of the other's blade on his buckler. So fierce was the blow that the sword point jammed in the coloured bullshide, and, bearing down on both shield and sword together, Cuchulain tore the weapon from his grasp, then flung sword and buckler in his face, and leapt

66

upon him, with his own sword biting deep upon the other's shield.

Forgall gave back towards the earth-cut rampart steps, snatching at his dagger, and so, the one with a long sword, the other with shield and dagger, they fought close-locked up the steps to the rampart walk, along the crest of the great turf bank, until Forgall felt at his back the raw timbers of the stockade. Lithe and desperate as a wild beast cornered, he doubled and twisted, seeking to break clear, but on all sides it seemed, he was hemmed in by the leaping sword-point of the Ulster hero. And at last, with a cry of furious despair, he too hurled his shield into his enemy's face, then turning, flung himself across the timber coping of the stockade.

He turned over as he fell, struck against the stone roots of the wall, and was flung off into the ditch, and among the furze scrub in the bottom of the ditch he lay still, spreadeagled in the light of the burning gateway.

In the forecourt of the Dūn the battle was slackening, and Cuchulain burst through it and ran towards the women's quarters, his sword still naked in his hand. The women were clustered like bats in the darkness, squealing somewhere at the back of the bower, all save Emer herself, and she had come out to the doorway and stood there waiting for him, with the last light of the burning thorn bushes shining in her eyes.

'I have won the place you bade me, among the Chariot Chieftains,' Cuchulain panted. 'I have slain my hundreds, and the harpers sing of me in the King's Hall. And so I come again—that also you bade me—but I could not wait for you to bid me to come in.'

'It seems indeed that you required but little bidding,' Emer said.

'I would have got none from your father, being not the King of Munster.'

'If you had been, it's not myself that would have been here waiting for you, for there's no wish on me to be Munster's Lady.'

'Come, then,' Cuchulain said, and catching her up across his shoulder, he turned and ran for the outer courtyard, where the chariots had been drawn back towards the gate, and the dead and wounded littered the ground, and the rest of Forgall's warriors, with no heart left in them, stood sullenly about the great weapon-stone in the midst of the courtyard, and the flaring light of torches that gilded the autumn mist fell upon cups of gold and silver and fine weapons and jewelled arm-rings piled within the chariots, for Cuchulain's men had not been idle. They greeted him with a shout as he made for his own chariot, and he set Emer down upon the floor of broad straps, and sprang in beside her, and cried to Laeg to whip up the team. 'Surely this has been a wedding to surpass all weddings, and as surely no bride ever brought with her a richer dowry!'

And with the six chariots behind him, he crashed out over the scattered embers of the thornwork gate, Emer clinging to the chariot rim beside him, and her dark hair flying like a storm cloud.

But the thing was not yet finished, for Forgall had a sister, and that night she raised a great war band on her own account in Meath, and came rushing after Cuchulain. Cuchulain heard their hooves behind him and caught the moonlight on their spears, and knew his own small battle-weary band to be many times outnumbered. But even as he knew it, his battle fury came upon him, and he brought his chariots wheeling about to face those who thundered on their track. And with the fight that followed, the turf was trampled to red mud, and the ford of Glondath ran blood. And turning again and again, he slew a hundred and more of the Meath men at every ford from Olney to the Boyne.

So for many years afterwards, if a man were telling of a battle that was especially sharp and bloody, he would say, 'Ach! It was like Cuchulain's wedding!'

7. Bricrieu's Feast

A YEAR or two after Cuchulain's wedding, Bricrieu of the Bitter Tongue made a feast in his Dūn and bade to it King Conor and all the Red Branch Heroes.

Conor was no fool. He knew that he could not refuse the invitation of one of his most powerful chieftains, for to do so would be to put an affront on the man before the eyes of all Ulster, that doubtless would be repaid full measure and running over, when the chance came. And he knew that to accept would also have its dangers, for Bricrieu was renowned as a trouble-maker, one who found in the stirring up of strife and ill will among his fellows the pleasure that other men found in battle or a day's hunting or their arms round a girl. So he said to the giver of the feast, looking him straightly in the eye, 'Bricrieu, you are no stranger to me. Which of my young warriors would you set against each other this time?'

'I?. My lord misjudges me. No such thought was in my mind.' Bricrieu shrugged and smiled. 'If I would stir up strife in the Red Branch, why should I go to the trouble of making a feast for them, when I could raise my little tempest as well in your hall as mine?'

'Nevertheless,' said the King, 'I should enjoy my meat more and drink with an easier mind in your hall if *you* were to feast elsewhere.'

'Somewhat strange, that must seem, in the giver of the feast?'

'Plead sickness. That should serve well enough,' the King said.

And Bricrieu knew that there was nothing left but to agree to Conor's terms with as smooth a face as might be.

But before he left Emain Macha for his own place, he contrived to meet Laery the Triumphant, who was one of the foremost warriors of the Red Branch, as he brought his chariot horses in from exercise. 'The sun and the moon on your path, Laery, winner of battles. Those are horses worthy of the Champion of Ireland! Indeed there are none swifter and stronger it seems to me in all Emain Macha—save perhaps for the Grey and the Black of Cuchulain's that he swears are horses of the Sidhe!'

For not long since, Cuchulain had chanced upon a great grey stallion splashing ashore out of the grey lough below Slieve Fuad, and had captured it after such a fight as shook Slieve Fuad to its roots. And in the same way, within three days, he had taken the great black water-horse of Lough Seinglend. And these were the Black Seinglend and the Grey of Macha, who were chief among his chariot horses from that time forward until his death-day.

'One day I will challenge Cuchulain to a race between his horses and mine,' said Laery, who loved his horses and could never bear to hear any other team praised above them.

'So? Maybe it would be better still if you were to challenge Cuchulain himself. For since his time in the Land of Shadows and his marriage to Emer he grows overproud, and would be the better for a lesson. Why, I have even heard that he claims to be the Champion of Ireland himself!' and Bricrieu laughed softly, with his hand on the chariot rim.

'There are two words as to that,' said Laery the Triumphant.

'Surely three. They are telling me that Conall Mac Finchoom makes the same claim—two mere striplings, and yourself a seasoned warrior. Ach well, at my house the Champion's Portion is always worth the having. When the roast boar is carried in tomorrow, bid your charioteer to rise and claim it for you, and we will see what follows!'

Laery leaned down towards him, suddenly fierce. 'There are some who shall go to feed the ravens, if my right is denied me!'

But Bricrieu only laughed a little tauntingly, as though he doubted it, and turned away, while Laery in a fury jabbed his bronze-tipped goad into the haunches of his team and sent them thundering on up the steep track towards the gates of Emain Macha.

Smiling still behind narrowed eyes, Bricrieu went in search of Conall, and found him testing a new birding bow by shooting at a tuft of kingfisher's feathers flying in the wind from a slim whippy hazel wand. When the arrow had thrummed away carrying one blue feather on its tip, Bricrieu said, 'Surely there is no hand quite like yours for the bow in all Ulster. It is no wonder that men begin to call you Conall of the Victories, for none dare face you in battle; not even Cuchulain, for all the hero-light that burns about his head.'

'It is as well, then, that we are not like to be standing against each other,' Conall said shortly, stooping for another arrow from the row he had set in the ground before him. 'For his shoulder has a good feel to it, when we stand together against a common foe; and a sorry thing it would be for foster brothers to be facing each other across the rims of their bucklers.'

'A sorry thing it is that all foster kin are not so loyal as Conall of the Victories,' Bricrieu said idly, and Conall turned to look at him, with the arrow already notched to his string. 'And what would be the meaning of that, then?'

'Nay, now, why should you pay any heed to the thing Cuchulain says? Yet it is true that all men believe by now you should have been declared Champion of Ireland.'

'It is mine to take when I will,' Conall said. 'But what is this that Cuchulain says?'

'That you would be claiming the Championship tomorrow, but that you are afraid of *him*.'

Conall's arrow flew wide and bedded in the turf walls of the Dūn, and his face darkened to a dusky red under the strong fair mane of hair. 'Truly it is in my mind that he has changed in the Land of Shadows. *Not* tomorrow but this very night I claim the Championship of Ireland!'

'Tomorrow! Wait until the night that you come with Conor to feast in my house. Then when the roast boar is brought in, bid your charioteer to rise and claim the Champion's Portion for your share; for the Red Branch Warriors should not be squabbling like starlings in the King's Hall.'

And he went on his way, well content, leaving Conall of the Victories hurt and raging, to gather up his arrow and tear down the pretty fluttering target and grind it into muddy pulp under his heel.

Cuchulain was sitting on the weathered stone well-curb in the courtyard of the women's quarters, laughing at some jest with one of Emer's maidens who had come to draw water. And when the girl had gone her way, Bricrieu sat himself down on the well-curb beside Cuchulain, and laughed also. 'Truly, being wed has not changed you! Not only are you our spear and shield against all enemies, the mightiest rampart of Ulster, but you must be holding every Ulster girl in the hollow of your hand, beside—whistling them as a bird off a tree. *They* would not deny you the Championship of Ireland!'

Cuchulain drew his black brows together. '*Who* then denies me the Championship of Ireland?'

'No, pay no heed. I let my tongue run away with me.'

'That poisoned tongue of yours never yet ran away with you,' Cuchulain said. '*Who* denies me the Championship of Ireland?'

Bricrieu pretended unwillingness, but when Cuchulain caught him by the shoulder to force it out of him, he told his lie. 'I thought you would have heard—Laery the Triumphant and Conall who men begin to call Conall of the Victories (forgetting, I suppose, how the High King of Tara died). Each of them has been putting it about that they are better men than you, that all your skill and strength are but a few shadow-tricks that Skatha taught you in the Land of Shadows, that you might make a fine showing before the Lady Emer, like a pied wagtail strutting before his hen.'

'You lie!' Cuchulain shouted. 'Even if Laery forgot his friendship he would never speak so of me behind my back; and Conall—Conall is my foster brother, my hearth-companion; as soon would I speak so of him as he speak so of me!'

He gave Bricrieu's shoulder a thrust that all but tipped him into the well, and Bricrieu jumped clear, rubbing the place where the young warrior's fingers had bitten, but smiling still with his lips.

'If you do not believe me, put it to the test! Tomorrow night when the Red Branch Warriors feast in my hall, bid your charioteer, when the roast boar is carried in, to rise and claim for you the Champion's Portion. Then see what these friends of yours will do! Only see!'

Cuchulain dashed his hand against the well-curb so that the blood sprang from his knuckles, before he could answer. 'I will do as you bid me, Adder Tongue! And I will see!'

And Bricrieu went home to his own place to make ready for the feast, promising himself an amusing evening.

On the night of the feast, Bricrieu welcomed the King and the Red Branch Heroes and their women when they entered his splendid hall at Dūn Drum, and then, excusing himself on the grounds of an old wound that was troubling him, withdrew from the hall, his own warriors with him, while the women of his household led Emer and her companions away to the women's quarters, for at Dūn Drum they followed the old custom and men and women did not eat together at feast times. But at the foot of the stair that led up to the private chambers behind the hall, he turned and looked back, smiling still. 'The Champion's Portion, you will find, is worth the having. Let it be given to the foremost hero in all Ulster.'

When he was gone, and the Red Branch Warriors were seated at the long tables down the sides of the hall, Bricrieu's slaves brought in the great chargers piled with oatcakes and curd, with mighty joints of oxen and deer meat and great silver salmon sizzling from the cooking spits; and last of all, borne proudly by four warriors, the great grizzly carcass of roast boar, whose right shoulder was the Champion's Portion.

The carriers came forward to do their part, and as the deep shoulder-cut was made amid a sudden silence in the uproar of the hall, the three charioteers of Laery and Conall and Cuchulain rose as one man, each to claim the Portion for his own lord.

For maybe the time that it would take an arrow to fly three hundred paces, the silence endured; and then tumult roared up through the hall, the three heroes shouting each for himself, and the others shouting for support of this man or that, until the King struck with all his force the silver rod in his hand upon the bronze forepost of the High Seat. And at the sound, like the throbbing clash of a great bell, all men fell silent, and stood looking towards the King.

But into the hush a new tumult arose, rushing nearer, the voices of many women raised in some quarrel of their own. 'It is in my mind that Bricrieu has been at his work again,' said Cathbad into his beard, and above the babble of women's voices, Emer's voice sounded, clear as the note of a silver trumpet, and her fists were beating on the postern-door. 'Cuchulain! Cuchulain! let me in!'

Cuchulain leapt to fling the bar aside, and dragged open the small heavy door, and Emer sprang through, between rage and laughter, and Fedelm the wife of Laery, and Conall's young bride Lendabair, that he had taken less than a moon ago, came thrusting after her and behind them all their companions.

Conor the King leaned forward in the High Seat, again striking the bronze forepost for silence, and demanded the meaning of the uproar.

Emer had been first into the hall, but Fedelm was the first to speak, flinging back the strong bay hair that had broken loose with her running, and fronting the whole hall with blazing pride. 'Look upon me, my Lord the King and all you warriors of Ulster. There is royal blood in me, and it is not for nothing that I am called Fedelm the Beautiful, as it is not for nothing that my husband is Laery the Triumphant, Laery of the Red Hand. Look upon me, and deny my right to walk first into the drink hall before all the other women of Ulster!'

Then Lendabair spoke out for herself; small she was and sweet, and cherished as a little pet bird, so that it was no wonder that she was called Lendabair the Favourite; and the hair of her soft and pollen-yellow so that sometimes the colour of it would make Cuchulain remember the yellow hair of the Princess Aifa. Now she spoke out fiercely enough, a small thing fighting for its own. 'I am not without some beauty too, and if I am not so fair as Fedelm, yet *I* have Conall of the Great Spear for my husband, Conall of the Victories! He goes with brave steps up to the spears of the fight, he brings his bright sword into the battle for Ulster, and none can stand against him. And proud he is, coming back to *me* afterwards, with the heads of the enemies in his hands! By right of Conall's war spear I should walk before all other women in Ulster!'

Then Emer spoke, last of all, fierce as a falcon, standing beside the Royal Fire, and more beautiful than all the rest. 'I am black, whereas my sisters here are bronze and golden, yet it is *I* who am called Emer of the Beautiful Hair, and they are not so fair as I am. There is no other woman has the joy of loving or the strength of loving that I have; and my Lord is Cuchulain, the Hound of Ulster, the Hound of Battle, the strong keeper of the gateway against all who come with spears. He fights from over the ears of his horses, he leaps like a salmon, he hews down whole armies; and I am the woman of the Hound of Ulster, and there is none worthy to walk before me among the women of the Red Branch or the women of Ulster or the women of all Ireland!'

'Now Bricriu has spent a happy evening,' Cathbad murmured to himself, but he scarcely meant to be heard, and none heard him, for now the men were joining in again, Laery and Conall and Cuchulain each shouting for his own wife now as well as for himself, and demanding of the King that he should make the choice. But Connor Mac Nessa, sitting alone on the High Seat, looking with frown-furrowed eyes into the faces of his three heroes and their three wives, knew that if he attempted to decide between them he would but make bitter enemies of the other two, and the struggle between themselves would still go on, unless their hot blood were first given time to cool. 'If my Queen had not died at young Follaman's birth,' he thought, 'I could have dealt with the women anyway, for they would not dare this wild squabbling if there were a Queen to walk before all three of them.'

Aloud, he said, 'This is a feast, not a battle ground! The Champion's Portion shall be divided among the three of you for this night, and later, we will put the thing to Maeve of Connacht, for being a stranger she may see with a clearer judgement than I among my own Red Branch kinsmen. Only this I say to you, that whatever her decision, you shall abide by it. And now, before the good meat grows cold——'

So Laery and Conall and Cuchulain sheathed their swords that had been out by that time, and sat down again, glaring at each other, but forced to abide by the King's ruling.

Only Bricriu, watching through a chink in the hanging was ill content at the way his evening's amusement had gone.

The feast at Dūn Drum lasted for three days and three

nights, with hunting by day and eating and drinking and harp music after dark, and during all that time the three heroes kept the peace between them but did not sit on the same bench nor drink from the same wine-cup. And on the fourth morning, when it was ended, they set out for Cruachan in Roscommon of Connacht to demand the judgement of Maeve and the King, as to which of them should be accounted the Champion of Ireland. And many of the Ulster warriors drove with them to see what befell.

And so by and by, sitting in her bower at Cruachan, beside the Hill of the Sidhe, Queen Maeve wondered, as Emer had done, to hear thunder from a clear sky, but her young daughter Findabair the Fair, who would be Queen after her, looked from the high window, and said, 'Mother, I see chariots coming.'

'Who drives in them?' demanded Maeve, looking up from combing her long straight fair hair beside the fire.

'In the first, a big man with blazing red-gold hair and beard. His cloak is purple as a thundercloud and he bears a javelin in his hand.'

'That sounds like Laery the Triumphant, the Storm of War,' said her mother. 'Sore trouble there will be in Cruachan, if he comes in anger! Who else?'

'In the second chariot I see a young fair-haired man with a skin as clear red and white as fresh blood spilled on snow. Chequered blue and crimson is his cloak, and his shield is brown with a bronze rim.'

'That sounds to be Conall of the Victories,' said Maeve. 'A sad day for Cruachan if he comes with his sword unsheathed!'

'There is a third chariot,' said Findabair, 'and the horses of its team are one grey as rain, and one black as midnight. The sods from their hooves fly in their wake like gulls behind the plough, and they cover the ground with the speed of a winter wind. And in that chariot stands a dark youth, his pleated tunic is crimson, and his cloak white and clasped with gold, and his shield is crimson with a silver rim and images of animals shine on it in gold. His hair is dark, and his look is dark also, yet it might well draw love, and assuredly it shoots fire; and the Hero light plays about his head.'

'That can only be the Hero Cuchulain,' said Maeve. 'Truly we shall be ground like fresh barley in the mill, if that one comes as an enemy.' And she rose and strode to the window beside her daughter and stood looking out, with her jewelled comb in her hand, and the long silver gilt hair falling either side of her long, fair, fierce face. And she saw the three chariots and behind them almost all of the Red Branch Warriors, the sound of the chariots and the horses' hooves as the dashing waves of the sea. 'I will send word to summon the King,' she said. 'We must welcome them fitly, and feast them finely, and if they are for trouble maybe that will turn their wrath away from Cruachan.'

And so the three heroes and their followers received a courteous welcome from Maeve, who was not wont to welcome strangers, and from Ailell, the King in her crowned shadow, and were feasted royally for three days and three nights, and at the end of that time, they demanded of Maeve and Ailell the judgement that they had come for. And Maeve and the King put them to three tests, by the three great cats of the Lordly Ones, and by the witches of a certain haunted valley, and by setting them to fight one at a time with Ailell's own foster father Ercol, who was a mighty magician skilled in all the ancient magic of red bronze and grey iron and blade's edge and shield's rim. And in all these tests and encounters, Cuchulain was the only one to overthrow his antagonists. But still Laery and Conall would not admit his right to the Championship of Ireland.

And now indeed Ailell grew perplexed, for he knew that he could no longer delay giving his judgement, and he knew that whichever of the three he named Champion, the two disappointed heroes would be his enemies from that day forward, and he was a peaceable man. He took counsel with Maeve in their chamber, and Maeve, who was as warlike as he was peaceable, listened to him with scorn and half-laughter on her pale face. 'What makes you think that the matter is for *your* judgement, little royal husband?' said she. For in Connacht the Queen was the Queen in her own right, but the King was the King only because he married her. But she was no fool, and though she scorned him for his caution, she knew in her heart that he was right to be anxious. So she said at last, 'Ach now, I spoke unthinking. But cease troubling for yourself and leave all to me. I promise you that I will so work it that all three of these Ulster madmen shall go from here satisfied.'

And summoning the King's armour-bearer, she bade him first to fetch certain things from the treasury, and then call to her Laery the Triumphant. And when the big ruddy man came ducking his head under the black and saffron painted lintel, she spoke for the King who sat uneasily beside her. 'Welcome to you, Laery the Triumphant. Well may men call you by that name, for you are the Champion of Ireland, and to you, my lord, I award the right to the Champion's Portion at any feast where you may be present.' And smiling, she took from the table and held out to him a cup of polished bronze with a silver bird inlaid upon one side. 'In token that it is so, take this, and show it to no man until you come again to King Connor at Emain Macha. Then show it before all men, and claim your right to the Championship of Ireland, and none, I think, will dispute it with you.'

So Laery stowed the cup in his breast, and went back to the great hall where the warriors were at their evening pastimes.

Then Maeve sent the armour-bearer for Conall, bidding him make sure that Laery and Cuchulain did not see. And to Conall also, she pretended to award the Championship of Ireland. But the cup that she gave him to show in proof was of whitest silver, inlaid with a bird of gold.

She waited until the other two had gone to their sleeping places before sending the armour-bearer for Cuchulain, who was sitting late over a game of chess with one of Ailell's warriors. But Cuchulain only twitched his shoulders as though a fly were troubling him, and would not come before he had finished and won the game.

Maeve grew angry at that, for she was the Queen of Connacht to her heart's core, and she sat tapping her foot on the hearth-stone, her eyes glittering bright and heavy under her lids while she waited, and twisted the ear of her favourite hound bitch between finger and thumb when it crept to her, until the poor brute yelped with surprise and pain. 'He shall have cause to regret one day that he kept Maeve of Connacht waiting!' she said.

But when at last Cuchulain appeared, she smiled upon him and greeted him as she had done the other two. 'Most welcome are you, Cuchulain of Ulster. But it is in my heart that you will never be lacking for welcome, save when you come in wrath, and then all men must quail before you as before the wrath of the High Gods themselves.' And she held out to him a third cup, wrought of yellow river gold, on which was a bird worked out in coral and carbuncle and blue enamel. 'Take this as a royal gift from Connacht to the Champion of all Ireland. Show it to no man until you come to King Conor at Emain Macha, then bring it out in the sight of all men. No other warrior, I think, will claim the right to the Championship hereafter.'

So Cuchulain stowed the golden cup in the breast of his tunic, and went out well content to the warriors' sleeping place.

Next morning the Red Branch Warriors took their leave of Maeve and Ailell, and set out for Emain Macha once again. And the chariots of Laery and Conall and Cuchulain drove in the forefront as by right, leaving the rest to follow in the cloud of their dust. But none of the three heroes asked the other two how they had fared, for each thought that he knew.

So they came again to Emain Macha, and that night there was feasting in the King's Hall to welcome the warriors home. And when the Champion's Portion was cut from the great roast and set aside, the feasting fell silent, and all men looked towards the three.

Then Laery rose in his place, and pulled from the breast of his tunic the bronze cup with the silver bird. 'I claim the Champion's Share!'

'By what right?' demanded Conor.

'By right of this cup, which Maeve of Connacht gave me to prove it!'

But before the words were out of his mouth, Conall of the Victories sprang to his feet, holding high the cup of silver with the bird of gold upon it. 'What of this, then, my lord the King? This that was given to *me* by the same Queen of Connacht, to prove *my* right to the Champion's Portion.'

And in the same instant Cuchulain also was on his feet and holding up for all to see, the cup of gold with its jewelled bird, which blazed in the firelit hall like the sun at midsummer. And standing there he said no word at all, but laughed until his laughter rang against the weapons on the walls.

8. The Championship of Ireland

THE quarrel began all over again, with Laery roaring in Cuchulain's face that he had bribed Maeve with a promise of his service to give him the golden cup. And though Conall said nothing as to that, he would no more accept the judgement than would Laery.

And when Conor the King could make himself heard, he said, coldly angry, 'Then here is my word. You shall go to Curoi of Kerry with this accursed claim; his sight is deeper and his powers older even than those of the Druids, and it may be that he can settle the thing once and for all. Meanwhile, let me hear no more of it.'

So next day the three heroes and their charioteers set out to lay the matter before Curoi the Lord of Kerry.

He was gone from home when they came clattering up the chariot way into the great Dūn on its coastwise headland where he had his palace. But Blanid his wife greeted them softly and warmly, lifting long eyelids at each in turn. And when she had heard what brought them to Dūn Curoi, she said 'Surely that is a thing that can be settled easily enough. But my lord will be three nights from home, and though he has left warriors set about me, I am a foolish woman and grow nervous when he is not by my side. Therefore, let me beg of you as a favour that each of you in turn will watch one night outside the stockade of the Dūn. In that way I shall feel safe.'

That night, when the time came for the warriors to seek their sleeping places, Laery, who was so much the eldest of the three, claimed the first watch, and took up his position outside the big thorn bush that closed the stockade. And Curoi's Queen went to her own chamber and lit a small fire in a brazier and fed it with strange and unholy things until it burned blue; and began to comb her crow-black hair and sing, weaving the charm that guarded the gate from all comers after nightfall—and other spells besides.

The night wore on quietly, and Laery was almost asleep leaning on his spear, when he saw a great shadow rising from the sea. Denser and darker and more menacing it grew, until it took the shape of a monstrous human figure, and the moonlight was blotted out behind its shoulders. And Laery saw with a thrill of horror that it carried two war spears whose shafts were branch-stripped oak trees.

'This is a bad night for Ulster,' said the Shadow Giant, and the voice of him boomed hollow as the sea in a cave. And on the word he flung both his spears at Laery the Triumphant; but they passed him by, one on either side, and stood quivering in the massive timber ramparts of the Dūn. Then Laery flung his own spears, and though they were better aimed, he might as well have thrown at a thundercloud as at the great mass towering over him; and with a boom of laughter the monster stooped and caught him up, gripping him so hard in one hand as almost to crush his ribs like egg-shells, and tossed him over the ramparts of the Dūn.

The tumult roused the warriors within, and they came running with Cuchulain and Conall at their head, and found Laery lying just inside the stockade, half dead with his bruises and bubbling for breath; and beyond the stockade the moonlight shining bright and unhindered as before.

The next night Conall took the watch, and all happened in the same way. And when the warriors came running to his aid, he told them of the fight with the giant, just as Laery had done, but like Laery, he could not bring himself to tell how the giant had tossed him contemptuously like a bundle of old rags over the wall. And so, knowing of the spell that Blanid the Queen set every night on the gateway, all men believed that both had jumped the high stockade.

The third night Cuchulain, the youngest, took up his watch outside the Dūn, and the Queen went to her chamber and made her blue fire and let down her black hair to weave the same spells as before, but this time she braided her hair into strange patterns and with each pattern she made another spell that she had not woven last night nor the night before, and little winds ran about the place and small shapeless things squeaked in the corners.

And Cuchulain, leaning on his spear before the gateway, had a quiet watch until midnight. And then he thought he saw nine grey shadows creeping towards him. 'Who comes?' he shouted. 'If you be friends, stand where you are; if you be foes, come on!'

And the nine shadow-warriors raised a great shout and sprang upon him all together, like hounds pulling down a stag; and he fought them all together, shouting his war-cry that made the very timbers of the Dūn shudder behind him, and slew them or drove them back into mist or hacked them into the ground. Then nine more of the shadows leapt upon him, and for the third time, nine more, and all of them Cuchulain dealt with; and then spent and breathless, sat down on a boulder beside the gate to rest.

And as he sat with his head sunk on his breast, he heard a great boom and crash of waves as though of a winter storm beating on the shore, though all about him the night was still. And looking up, he saw a monstrous dragon threshing up from the water. High and higher into the air it rose in an arching blaze of fearful glory like a shooting star, and its wings spread half across the sky as it sank with terrible open jaws towards Cuchulain.

Cuchulain's weariness dropped from him like a threadbare cloak, and he sprang to his feet, then made the Hero's Salmon Leap straight up to meet the winged terror, and thrust the full length of his arm down its throat. It was as though his arm was engulfed to the shoulder in living fire, and the hot stinking breath of the creature beat in his face. His hand found the huge pulsing heart and tore it out by the roots.

The monster fell out of the air, black blood bursting from its mouth, and the blaze of its eyes dying out like the red gleeds of a sinking fire. Cuchulain sprang upon the body of the dead monster, and smiting off its head, set it on the pile of three times nine grey snarling warriors' heads he had raised already. And again he sank down on the boulder.

It was almost dawn when he became aware of the shadow coming up from the sea that both Laery and Conall had encountered. Cuchulain rose to his feet and stood waiting while the shadow darkened and took on giant shape.

'This is a bad night for Ulster,' said the shape, raising the first of the two great spears.

'Yet it may be a worse night for you!' Cuchulain cried.

And the two spears came whistling one after the other, missing him as narrowly as they had missed Laery and Conall, to crash deep into the timber walls of Dūn Curoi; and the monster stooped to grapple with him. But in the same instant Cuchulain sprang up, sword in hand, and leaping as high as the giant's head, flashed in a mighty blow that brought him tumbling to his knees. The giant roared out in a great anguished voice, and with the cry still hanging in the air, was gone like a curl of wood-smoke that the wind whips away.

The first faint light of dawn was broadening over the sea, and Cuchulain knew that there would be no more comers that night, and weary as he was, he thought to go back into the Dūn and rest. But the spells that held the gateway would not yield until the first rays of the sun touched the threshold, and if, as he believed, the other two had leapt the stockade, then so could he. Twice he tried the leap, and twice, with his weariness on him, he failed; and then a great rage rose in him that he could not do what his comrades had done, and with the rage, his utmost strength came upon him, and the Hero light began to flicker like summer lightning about his head, and he took a little run, and vaulting on his spear, went up and over, so high and far that the leap carried him not merely across the wall but into the heart of the Dūn, and he landed on his feet again in the inner court, on the very threshold of Curoi's hall.

He sank down on the door sill, and leaning against the painted doorpost, heaved a great slow sigh.

And Curoi's wife came out from the hall behind him and stooped to touch his shoulder, letting the darkness of her hair trail all across his face. 'That is the sigh of a weary conqueror, not of a beaten man,' she said. 'Come in now, and eat and rest.'

Later, she showed to all three the pile of heads that lay at her gate and said, 'Those are beside the Shadow Giant, who leaves no trace. Now are you content to yield to Cuchulain the Champion's Portion?' she said.

But still the other two would not yield the victory, Laery out of hot jealousy and Conall because by that time he was growing ashamed, and shame always made him the more stubborn. 'No!' said Laery. 'And how should we be content? All men know that Cuchulain was fathered within the Hollow Hills. His own kin among the Lordly People have aided him in this; therefore the contest is an unfair one.'

'Then there is no more that I can do to help you settle the thing,' said Blanid; and she looked just as any other woman whose patience is worn into holes, save that the dark hair on the head of her lifted and crackled like the fur of a black cat that is stroked the wrong way when there is thunder in the air. 'Go home now to Emain Macha, and wait there until my Lord Curoi himself brings you his judgement. But see that you keep the peace with each other while you wait, and whatever the judgement of Curoi may be, see that you accept it, lest Ulster become a laughing stock to Munster and Leinster and Tara and Connacht, for this child's quarrel among her greatest heroes!'

So the three returned to King Conor with the quarrel still unhealed between them, but they kept the peace as Curoi's wife had commanded.

And the days went by and the days went by with no word from Curoi of Kerry. And then one evening when all the Red Branch Warriors were at meat in the King's Hall, save for Conall who was off hunting and his foster brother Cuchulain who had driven down to his own lands of Murthemney to see how the work went on the new house that his men were raising within the old ring-banks of Dūn Dealgan, the door flew open as though at a great blast from the first of the winter gales that was howling like a wolf pack outside. And as all eyes leapt towards it, a terrible figure strode through into the wind-scurried firelight. A creature like a man but taller than any mortal man, horrible to see, and with the yellow eyes of a wolf that glared about the hall as he came. He was clad only in wolfskins roughly sewn together, and a grey mantle over them, and shaded himself from the light of fire and torches with a young oak tree torn up by the roots; and in his free hand he swung a mighty axe with a keen and cruelly shining edge.

Up the hall strode the horrifying visitor, where every warrior had sprung to his feet, and leaned himself against the massive carved and painted roof-tree beside the central hearth.

'Who are you?' asked Cethern Son of Findtan, striving to make a jest of it. 'Are you come to be our candlestick, or would you burn the house down? Go farther down the hall, my large and hairy friend.'

'Men call me Uath the Stranger, and I am come for neither of those purposes,' returned the giant, in a voice as terrible as his looks. 'I come to see whether, here among the Red Branch Warriors of Ulster, I may find the thing that I have failed to find elsewhere in all Ireland.'

'And what would that be?' demanded Conor the King.

'A man to keep the bargain that he makes with me.'

'And this bargain? Is it then so hard to keep?'

The stranger hunched his great skin-clad shoulders. 'It would seem so.' Then he swung up the great axe he carried, and held it high, so that all might see the glitter of the firelit blade. 'Behold this axe of mine, is she not fair? But always she is hungry—hungry for the blood of men. Any man bold enough to grasp her tonight may use her to cut my head from my shoulders—provided that he comes here to meet me again tomorrow night that I may return the blow.'

A low murmur of voices, half awed, half angry, sounded all down the crowded benches of the hall; and the stranger looked round him with eyes that blazed like a wolf's when they catch the edge of the firelight. 'The Heroes of the Red Branch are accounted foremost in all Ireland for courage, honour, strength and truth; therefore, let you prove it by finding me, from among you, a man to keep this bargain with me—any man save the King.' His voice rose to a roar like that of a gale among trees. 'If you fail to find me such a champion, then must I say before all men that Ulster has lost her courage and is dishonoured!'

Hardly had he made an end than Laery sprang from his seat. 'Not yet is Ulster without a champion! Give me the axe, and kneel down, fellow!'

'Not so fast! Not so fast, manikin!' Uath the Stranger laughed and began to caress the gleaming axe blade, murmuring over it in a tongue that was strange to all men there. Then handing the weapon to Laery, he knelt and laid his neck over a mighty oak log beside the fire. Leary stood over him, swinging the great axe to test its weight and balance, then brought it crashing down with such force that the stranger's head leapt apart from his body, and the blade bit deep into the log.

Then a horrified gasp broke from all beholders, for as Laery the Triumphant stood back, the body of the stranger twitched, then rose and pulled the axe from the block and picked up its own head from where it had rolled against the hearthstone, and strode down the hall and out into the wild night; and it seemed that the very flames of the torches burned blue behind his passing.

And Laery stood beside the fire, looking as though he had been struck blind.

Next evening the Red Branch Warriors sat at supper in the King's Hall. But they ate little and talked little; and all eyes were turned towards the door. It burst open as before, and in strode Uath the Stranger, with his hideous head set as firmly as ever on his shoulders, and the huge axe swinging in his hand.

As before, he came and leaned against the roof-tree and looked about him with yellow eyes under his brows. 'Where is the warrior with whom I last night made a bargain?'

And King Conor Mac Nessa demanded also of his warriors, 'Where is Laery the Triumphant?'

And up and down the benches the warriors looked at each other, but no man had seen Laery the Triumphant that evening.

'So not even among the flower of the Ulster Warriors is there one to keep his word! Never think again to hold your heads high among the Chariot Chiefs of the world, oh small whipped curs of Ulster who cannot count among you one champion whose honour counts as much with him as a whole skin.'

Conall had returned from his hunting and was in the hall that night, and he sprang up, crying, 'Make the bargain afresh, oh Uath the Stranger; make it with me, and you shall not have cause a second time to cry shame on the men of Ulster!'

So the stranger laughed again, and made his magic in a strange tongue, and knelt for Conall as he had knelt for Laery. And again when the blow had been struck, he rose and took up the axe and his own severed head and strode out into the night.

The next evening Conall took his accustomed place among the warriors at supper, white and silent, but determined on his fate. Only when the door burst open as before, and the dreadful figure came striding up the hall, his own courage broke, for it was one thing to die in the red blaze of battle, with company on the journey, and quite another to lay one's head on the block in cold blood, for such an executioner; and he slipped down behind the benches and made for the small postern doorway of the hall.

So when Uath the Stranger called for Conall of the Victories, there was no answer save the click of the falling door pin.

Then Uath looked about him at the shamed and angry faces of King and warriors. 'A pitiful thing it is to see how men such as the Red Branch Warriors hanker after a great name and yet lack the courage to deserve it! Great warriors indeed you are, who cannot furnish forth *one* man to keep his faith with me! Truly even Cuchulain, though he is nothing but a boy that must stain his chin with bramble juices when he wishes to seem a man, one would think too proud to behave as these two mighty heroes have behaved!'

Cuchulain rose from his place among the Royal kinsmen, and flung his defiance down the hall in a trumpet shout, 'Young I may be, Uath the Stranger, but I keep my word!'

'Come you and prove it, then,' said Uath the Stranger, 'for it is one thing to say and another to do!'

And with a great cry Cuchulain came leaping down the hall and seized the axe from the giant's hand, and springing up from the floor, smote the Stranger's head from his shoulders without even waiting for him to kneel down.

Uath the Stranger lurched like an oak tree in a gale, then steadied, and took back the axe from Cuchulain as though there were nothing odd in the way of it at all, and strode after his head which had bounced like a great hurley ball far off under one of the benches; and so walked down the hall and out into the night, the flames of the torches burning blue behind him.

Next night Cuchulain took his usual place among the warriors. And though the rest, watching him, saw that he was very white and that he scarcely touched the food but drank more than usual of the mead, he had not the look of a man who would take one step backward from the thing that he had come to meet.

Late into the evening, once again the wind rose and the door burst open, and in strode Uath the Stranger, wearing his terrible majesty like a cloud of darkness upon him, and cried out, striking the butt of his axe against the roof-tree, 'Where

is Cuchulain? Let him come out to me now, if he would keep his bargain!'

Cuchulain rose in his place and stepped forward. 'I am here.'

'The sadness is in your voice,' Uath said, 'and who shall wonder. Let it be a comfort to you when the axe falls, that you have redeemed the honour of Ulster.' He fingered the axe edge with head cocked, as a harper tuning his instrument. 'Kneel down, now.'

Cuchulain cast one last look round the great hall, seeing Emer's white stone-still face among the women's benches, and the faces of the King, and his friends, and the hounds that he had loved. Then he knelt and laid his head on the great log beside the fire.

'Stretch out your neck farther,' said the voice of Uath, tree-tall above him.

'You are playing with me as a cat plays with a bird!' Cuchulain said angrily. 'Kill me swiftly, for I did not torment you with waiting last night!'

The stranger swung up his axe until the butt of it broke through the rafters with a crash like that of a great tree falling in a storm, then brought it sweeping down in a glittering arc; and the crash of the blow seemed to make the whole hall jump on its foundations. And of the men watching, some covered their eyes, and some could not look away from the horror.

But the young warrior knelt perfectly unharmed, and beside him, no longer the hideous stranger, stood Curoi of Kerry, leaning on his great axe which had bitten deep into the paved floor, smashing the flagstones within a hand's breadth of Cuchulain's head.

'Did I not send you the word through my Queen that I would bring you my decision by and by?' said Curoi. 'Rise up now, Cuchulain.' And as Cuchulain got slowly to his feet and looked about him, as though he were not sure even now that his head was secure upon his shoulders, he said, 'Is the thing still in doubt? Here stands the Champion of all the Heroes of Ireland. The only one among you all, who dared to keep his bargain with death because he gave his word. There is none among the Heroes of Ulster to equal the Hound for courage and truth and honour, and therefore to him I adjudge the Championship and the Champion's Portion at any feast where he may be present, and to Emer his wife, the first place among the princesses of Emain Macha.' For an instant he seemed almost as terrible as Uath the Stranger had been. 'This is the word of Curoi of Kerry, and woe to any warrior who shall dispute it!'

And as he spoke, suddenly it was only his voice that was there, and the firelight shining through the place where he had been. And with the last words spoken, nothing was left of Curoi at all, only the foredoor of the hall crashed shut as though a great wind had blown it to.

For the time that a man might take to draw seven breaths, no one spoke or moved in the hall of Conor the King. And then men began to leave their places and crowd round Cuchulain where he still stood beside the hearth.

Laery came with the rest, and Conall of the Victories to set his arm about Cuchulain's shoulders.

'Why did you speak evil words of me to such as Bricrieu Poison Tongue?' Cuchulain said.

And in the same instant Conall said, 'Why did you speak poison of me to Bricrieu the Gadfly? I would not have spoken so of *you*.'

And Laery grumbled in his russet beard, 'Young cubs, you are, to say scornful things of me to that bird of ill omen, Bricrieu! But I am older, and should have had some wisdom.'

And they looked from one to another in sudden understanding. 'Bricrieu! Of course!' and then began to laugh, and the laughter spread all up and down the hall and broke in waves of mirth against the rafters.

And from that time forward, Cuchulain was acknowledged by all men to be Champion of all the Heroes of Ireland.

9. Deirdre and the Sons of Usna

NOW when Cuchulain and Emer had been together a few years in the sunny house that he had built at Dūn Dealgan, a great sorrow and the shadow of a great threat fell upon Ulster. But the beginning of that wild story was long before, in the year that Cuchulain first went to the Boys' House.

In that year a certain Ulster chieftain called Felim made a great feast for the King and the Red Branch Warriors. And when the feasting was at its height, and the Greek wine was going round and the harp song shimmering through the hall, word was brought to Felim from the women's quarters that his wife had borne him a daughter.

The warriors sprang to their feet to drink health and happiness upon the bairn, and then the King, half laughing, bade Cathbad, who was with him, to foretell the babe's fortune and make it a bright one. Cathbad went to the door of the hall and stood for a long while gazing up at the summer stars that were big and pollen-soft in the sky, and when he came back into the torchlight there was shadow in his face, and for a while he would not answer when they asked him the meaning of it. But at last he said, 'Call her Deirdre, for that name has the sound of sorrow, and sorrow will come by her to all Ulster. Bright-haired she will be, a flame of beauty; warriors will go into exile for her sake, and many shall fight and die because of her, yet in the end she shall lie in a little grave apart by herself, and better it would be that she had never been born.'

Then the warriors would have had the babe killed there and then, and even Felim, standing grey-faced among them, had

nothing to say against it; but Conor Mac Nessa, his own
Queen having died a while since in bearing Follaman their
youngest son, had another thought and he said, 'Ach now,
there shall be no slaying, for clearly this fate that Cathbad reads
in the stars can only mean that some chieftain of another province or even maybe of the Islands or the Pict Lands over the
water will take her for his wife and for some cause that has to
do with her, will make war on us. Therefore, she shall grow up
in some place where no man may set eyes on her, and when
she is of age to marry, then I myself will take her for Queen.
In that way the doom will be averted, for no harm can come to
Ulster through her marriage to me.'

So Conor Mac Nessa took charge of the child, and gave her
to Levarcham his old nurse who was one of the wisest women
in all Emain Macha. And in a hidden glen of Slieve Gallion he
had a little house built, with a roof of green sods so that above
ground it would look no more than one of the little green
hillocks of the Sidhe, and a turf wall ringing it round, and a
garden with apple trees for shade and fruit and pleasure. And
there he set the two of them, to have no more sight of men,
save that once a year his own most trusted warriors should
bring them supplies of food and clothing, until the child was
fifteen and ready to become his Queen.

So in the little secret homestead with her foster mother,
Deirdre grew from a baby into a child and from a child into a
maiden, knowing no world beyond the glen, and seeing no
man in all that time, for every year when the warriors came,
Levarcham would shut her within doors until they were gone
again. Every year the King would send her some gift, a silver
rattle hung with tiny bells of green glass, a coral-footed dove
in a wicker cage, a length of wonderfully patterned silk that
had come in a ship from half the world away. 'What *is* a ship?'

said Deirdre to her foster mother, 'and how far is half the world away? Could I get there if I set out very early in the morning and walked all day until the first stars came out?' And at that, Levarcham grew anxious, knowing that her charge was beginning to wonder about the world beyond the glen.

In the year that she was fourteen, her gift was a string of yellow amber that smelled fragrant as a flower when she warmed it between her hands, and that year the King brought it himself, and came with it into the house under the sheltering turf. And so for the first time, he saw Deirdre, and he with the first grey hairs already in his beard. And sorrow upon it, from that moment he gave her his heart's love, and she could never be free of it again.

That was in the summer, and before the cuckoo was gone, and before the last scarlet leaves fell from the wild cherry trees, and before the first snow came, the King returned to the glen for another sight of Deirdre. She knew that she was to be his Queen, but 'twas little enough that meant to her for good or ill, for it was a thing that belonged to the outside world, and the outside world as yet seemed very far away.

And then one winter night the outside world came to her threshold.

A wild night it was, with the wind roaring up through the woods and the sleety rain of it hushing across the turf roof, and Deirdre was sitting at old Levarcham's feet, spinning saffron wool by the light of the burning peats, when she thought she heard a strange cry, mingled with the voices of the storm, and lifted her head to listen. 'What was that, my Mother?'

'Only a bird calling to its mate through the storm. Nothing that need concern you,' said Levarcham.

But the cry came again, nearer now, and Deirdre said, 'It

sounded like a human voice—and the voice of one in sore trouble.'

'It is only the wild geese flying over. Bide by the fire and go on spinning.'

And then between gust and gust of the wind there came a fumbling and a thumping against the timbers of the small strong door, and the voice cried, 'Let me in! In the name of the sun and the moon let me in!'

And heedless of the old woman crying out to stop her, Deirdre leapt up and ran to unbar and lift the rowan-wood pin; and the door swung open and the wind and rain leapt in upon her, and with the wind and the rain, a man stumbled into the house place, and his sodden cloak like spread wings about him, as though he were indeed some great storm-driven bird.

He aided Deirdre to force shut the door. And as he came into the firelight that shone on his rain-drenched hair that was black as a crow's wing and on his face, and on the great height of him, Levarcham took one look at him and said, 'Naisi, Son of Usna, it is not the time to be bringing up the year's supplies. You have no right in this place.'

'Myself not being the King,' Naisi said, and let his sodden cloak fall from his shoulders, though indeed he was as wet within it as without. 'A storm-driven man has a right to any shelter that opens to him.'

'And shall we have your brothers at the door next? Seldom it is that you three are apart!'

'We have been hunting together, but Ardan and Ainle turned homeward before I did,' said the tall man, and swayed. 'Give me leave to sit by your fire until the storm sinks, for I have been lost and wandering a long while until I saw your light and—it is weary I am.'

'Ach well, if you tell no man that you have been here,

there'll be no harm done, maybe,' said Levarcham. 'Sit, then, and eat and drink while you're here, for by the looks of you, if I turn you away now, the Red Branch will be one fewer by morning.'

So Naisi sank down with a sigh upon the piled sheepskins, almost into the warm peat ash, and sat there with hanging head, the sodden hunting-leathers steaming upon him. Deirdre brought barley bread, and curd from their little black cow, and a cup of pale Greek wine, and set all beside him. He had been careful until then not to look at her, but when she gave the cup into his hands, he looked up to thank her; and having looked, could not look away again. And Deirdre could not look away either.

And Levarcham, watching both of them out of her small bright eyes, while she went on with Deirdre's abandoned spinning, saw how it was with them, and how the blood came back into Naisi's face that had been grey as a skull, and how the girl's face answered his, and thought to herself, 'Trouble! Grief upon me! I see such trouble coming, for there's no grey in *his* beard, and she with all the candles lit behind her eyes for him! I should have turned him away to die in the storm.' But there was a little smile on her, all the same, for despite her loyalty to Conor Mac Nessa who had been her nursling, she had felt it always a sad thing that Deirdre should be wed to the King who was old enough to have fathered her.

After that, King Conor was not the only one to come visiting Deirdre, for again and again Naisi would come to speak with her, and Levarcham knew that she should tell this to the King, but the time went by and the time went by and she listened to Deirdre's pleading and did not tell him.

Then one evening when the wind blew over the shoulder of Slieve Gallion from the south and the first cold smell of spring was in the air, Deirdre said to Naisi when it was time for him to go, 'Let you take me with you, and not leave me to be Queen beside a King that has grey hairs in his beard.'

And Naisi groaned. 'How can I do as you ask? I that am one of the King's own bodyguard, his hearth companion?'

And he went away, vowing in his heart that he would come no more to the turf house in the hidden glen. But always he came again, and always Deirdre would plead, 'Naisi, Naisi, take me away with you, it is you that I love. I have given no troth to the King for none has ever been asked of me, and it is yours that I am.'

For a long while he held out against her, and against his own heart. But at last, when the apple trees behind the house were white with blossom, and Deirdre's wedding to the King no more than a few weeks away, the time came when he could hold out no longer. And he said, 'So be it then, bird-of-my-heart, there are other lands across the sea and other kings to serve. For your sake I will live disgraced and die dishonoured, and not think the price high to pay, if you love me, Deirdre.'

In the darkness of the next night he came with horses, and with Ardan and Ainle his brothers; and they carried off both Deirdre and Levarcham, for the old woman said, 'Grief upon me! I have done ill for your sakes, and let you not leave me now to the King's wrath!'

They fled to the coast and took ship for Scotland, and there Naisi and his brothers took service with the Pictish King. But after a while the King cast his looks too eagerly in Deirdre's direction, and they knew that the time had come to be moving on again.

After that they wandered for a long while, until they came at last to Glen Etive, and there they built a little huddle of turf bothies on the loch shore, and the men hunted and Deirdre and the old nurse cooked for them and spun and wove the wool of their few mountain sheep; and so the years went by.

And in all those years, three, maybe, or four, Conor Mac Nessa made no sign, but sat in his palace at Emain Macha, and did not forget. And from time to time some ragged herdsman or wandering harper would pass through Glen Etive and beg shelter for the night, and afterwards return to Conor the King and tell him all that there was to tell of Deirdre and the sons of Usna—and they thinking themselves safe hidden all the while.

At last it seemed to the King, from the things told him by his spies, that the sons of Usna were growing restless in their solitudes; their thoughts turning back, maybe, to the life in a king's hall, and the feasting and the fighting to which they had been bred. Then he sent for Conall of the Victories, and Cuchulain, and old Fergus Mac Roy, and said to them, 'It is in my mind that the sons of Usna have served long enough in exile, and the time comes to call them home.'

'In friendship?' said Cuchulain, for he had never judged his kinsman one who would easily forgive a wrong, even after so long a time.

'In friendship,' said the King. 'I had a fool's fondness for the girl, but that is over long since. More it means to me to have the young men of my bodyguard about me. Therefore, one of you three shall go to Glen Etive, and tell them that the past is past, and bring them again to Emain Macha.'

'And which of us three?' said Conall.

And the King considered, turning his frowning gaze from one to the other. 'Conall, what would you do if I were to choose you, and harm came to them through me, after all?'

And Conall returned his gaze as frowningly. 'I should know

how to avenge them, and my own honour that would lie dead with them.'

'That sounds like a threat,' said the King, 'but it makes no matter, since the question is but an empty one.' And he turned to Cuchulain.

'I can answer only as Conall has answered,' Cuchulain said, 'but I think that after the revenge was over, men would no longer call me the Hound of Ulster but the Wolf of Ulster.' And he looked long and hard into the King's eyes. 'Therefore, it is as well, I think, that it is not myself that you will be sending to bring home the sons of Usna.'

'No, it is not yourself, but Fergus Mac Roy that I shall send,' said Conor the King. And Fergus, who was no fool in the general way of things, was so filled with gladness—for he loved Naisi and his brothers almost as much as he did Cuchulain, as much as he loved his own sons, and his heart had wearied for them in their exile—that he lost his judgement and he did not see the look that Cuchulain had turned upon the King.

So Fergus went down to the coast and took ship for Scotland and at last and at last he came on a quiet evening to the cluster of green bothies on the shore of Glen Etive; and when Naisi and his brothers, who were but just returned from their hunting, saw him drawing near along the shore, they came racing to meet him and fling their arms about his shoulders, greeting him and marvelling at his coming, and demanding what would be the latest news out of Ireland.

'The news out of Ireland is this,' said Fergus, as they turned back towards the bothies together. 'That Conor the King has put from his mind the thing that happened four springs ago between you and Deirdre and himself, and can no longer get the full pleasure of his mead-horn nor the full sweetness of harp song unless you return in friendship to enjoy them with him as you used to do.'

Now at this the three brothers set up a shout, for they were as joyful to hear his news as he was to tell it. But Deirdre, who had come from the bothies to join them, said, 'The sons of Usna do well enough here in Scotland. Let you be welcome here at our hearth, and then go back and tell King Conor that.'

'We do well enough here,' said Naisi, 'but each man does best in the land that bred him, for it is there that the roots of his heart are struck.'

'Ah, Naisi, Naisi, I have seen you and Ardan and Ainle growing weary of this happy Glen Etive; I know how you have longed for the King's Hall, and to be driving again like the wind behind the swift horses of Ulster. Yet I have had evil dreams of late and there is a shadow on my heart.'

'Deirdre, what is it that you are afraid of?'

'I scarcely know,' said Deirdre. 'I find it hard to believe in the King's forgiveness. What safeguard have we if we give ourselves back into his power?'

And Fergus Mac Roy said, 'Mine. And I think that no king in all Ireland would dare to violate that.'

Then while they ate the evening meal about the peat fire in the house place, Naisi laughed at her for her fears, swaggering a little with his thumbs in his belt, because the King had sent for him to come back to his old place again. And next day they gathered up all that they had of goods and gear, and went down to the coast, to where the ship that had brought Fergus from Ireland lay waiting on the tide line. And the bothies by the loch shore were left empty and forsaken.

The rowers bent to their oars and the long corach slipped seaward; and sitting in the stern with old Levarcham against her knee, Deirdre looked back past the man at the steering oar towards the shores of Scotland, and a lament rose in her, and would not be held back.

'My love to you, oh land of Alban; pleasant are your harbours and your clear green-sided hills. Glen Archan, my grief! High its hart's tongue and bright its flowers; never were young men lighter hearted than the three sons of Usna in Glen Archan. Glen-da-Rua, my grief! Glen-da-Rua! Sweet is the voice of the cuckoo in the woods of Glen-da-Rua. Glen Etive, my grief! Ochone! Glen Etive; it was there I built my first house, and slept under soft coverings with Naisi's hand beneath my head. And never would I have left you, Glen Etive, but that I go with Naisi my love.'

Scarcely had they set foot in Ulster once more, when Baruch, a veteran of the Red Branch, came to meet them, and bade Fergus, as an old friend, to feast with him that night in his Dūn close by. And with him were Fergus's two sons, Illan the Fair and Buinne the Red, come to greet him on his return. Now Fergus did not know that the King had ordered that feast, but he knew that his oath to Conor Mac Nessa bound him to bring Deirdre and the sons of Usna straight from their landing place to Emain Macha, and he tried to win clear of the thing, saying that he could not turn aside from his way until he had brought Deirdre and the three brothers under safe conduct to the King's presence. But Baruch would not be denied, and bade him remember that his geise forbade him ever to refuse when bidden to a feast, and so at last despite Deirdre's pleading (for no warrior might go against his geise) he bade his sons to take charge of the party, and himself went with Baruch.

When the six of them drew near to Emain Macha, Deirdre said, 'See now, how it will be. If Conor the King bids us to his own hall and his own hearth-side, then he means us no ill; but if we are lodged apart in the Red Branch Hostel, then grief upon us! For all that I fear will come to pass.'

And when they came into the Royal Dūn they were lodged in the Red Branch Hostel, to wait until the King should send for them. And Deirdre said, without hope of being heeded, 'Did I not tell you how it would be?'

But Naisi only laughed and held her warm in his arms, saying, 'Soon the King will send for us in friendship, and all things will be as they used to be.'

But first the King sent for old Levarcham, and she went and made her peace with him where he sat moodily in his sleeping-chamber with his favourite hound at his feet. And he asked her how it was with Deirdre, and if her beauty was on her yet, after so many years in the wilderness.

'Ach now, what would you be expecting? Life in the wilderness deals hardly with a woman,' said Levarcham. 'The skin that was so white is brown now, and the wind has chapped her lips and the sun has faded her hair. Her beauty is all gone from her and if you were to see her now you would think her any farmer's woman.'

'Then I will not send for her when I send for the sons of Usna,' said the King, and he sighed. 'Since Naisi has had her beauty, let him keep her. I will not see her again.'

But when Levarcham had been gone a while he began to doubt in his heart whether she had told him the truth, and he called to him his shield-bearer, and said, 'Go you and find some means to look secretly at the woman that is in the Red Branch Guest House, and come back and tell me whether she is yet fair to look upon.'

So it was that when those within the Guest House were taking their ease after the evening meal, Deirdre and Naisi playing chess together while the others lay about the fire, Ardan cried out suddenly and sprang to his feet, pointing to the high window in the gable wall. And looking where he pointed, Naisi saw the face of the King's shield-bearer peering in; and he caught up a golden chessman from the board and flung it at him, and it caught him in the face and struck out his left eye.

The man loosed his hold on the window-ledge with a sobbing cry and dropped to the ground, and ran and stumbled back to King Conor with his bloody face in his hands.

'The woman in the Red Branch Guest House is the fairest that ever I have seen. And if Naisi Son of Usna had not seen me and put out my eye with the fling of a golden chess piece, it is in my heart that I would have been clinging to the window-ledge and gazing at her still.'

Then Conor Mac Nessa in a black fury came out into his great hall and shouted to his warriors that were feasting there to be out and bring the three sons of Usna before him, he cared not whether alive or dead, or if they must pull down the Red Branch Hostel timber by timber and turf by turf to do it; for they were traitors that had done him foul wrong in the matter of the woman Deirdre.

The warriors sprang from the benches and snatched up their weapons and ran out, shouting, tossing the war-cry to and fro among them, and some, in passing the fires, pulled out flaming branches and whirled them above their heads as they ran, and so Naisi and the rest within the Hostel saw the red flicker of the firebrands through the high windows, and heard the shouting. And Deirdre cried out, wild as a storm-driven bird, 'Treachery! Naisi, Naisi, I told you that I feared evil, but you would not listen to me!'

And in the same moment Naisi himself had leapt to drop the mighty bar across the door.

'Look to the windows! The windows, my brothers, and you sons of Fergus who came here with us in his stead!'

And each catching up their weapons, they ran to their places, and for a breath of time there was stillness in the hall. Then the great voice of Celthair Son of Uthica cried to them from before the door. 'Out with you, thieves and rievers! Come out to us now, and bring with you the woman you stole from the King!'

And standing within the door Naisi shouted back, 'Neither thieves nor rievers are we, for the woman came to me for love and of her own wish; and with me and with my brothers she shall remain, though every champion of the Red Branch comes against us!'

But it was not long that they could hold the Hostel, for someone shouted, 'Burn them out, then, we have the fire-brands!' And the shouting rose to a roar, and the warriors thrust their blazing branches under the thatch. And Deirdre cried out at the sight of the red flame running among the rafters, and the hall began to fill with smoke.

Then Naisi said, 'It is time to unbar the door, for it is better to die by the cold blade than the choking reek of fire!'

So they heaved up the bar and flung wide the door, and leapt to meet the King's warriors who were ready for them like terriers at the mouth of a rat hole. A great fight there was, about the threshold of the Red Branch Guest House, and many of the warriors of Ulster fell before the blades of the sons of Usna and the sons of Fergus Mac Roy. And in the fighting Illan the Fair got his death, but to Buinne the Red a worse thing befell, for the King contrived to have him surrounded and brought living out of the fight, and bought him with the promise of much land.

Then with the Red Branch Hostel roaring up in flames behind them, Naisi and his brothers linked their three shields together and set Deirdre in the midst of them, and so made a great charge to break through the press of Conor's warriors. And spent and wounded as they were they might yet have won clear, but that Conor Mac Nessa, seeing how it was, bade certain of his Druids to make a strong magic against them, and the Druids made the seeming of a dark wild sea that rose and rose around the island of linked shields, so that the sons of Usna were fighting against the waves of it more than the warriors of the King's Guard. And Naisi, feeling the cold buffeting of the sea rise higher about him and seeing the white hissing break of the waves against their linked shields, caught Deirdre up on to his shoulder to save her from the sea. And they were choking and half drowned, while all the while, to all men save themselves, the King's forecourt was dry as summer drought in the red glare of the burning Hostel.

So at last their strength failed them and the Red Branch Warriors closed about them and struck the swords from their hands, and took and bound them and dragged them before King Conor where he stood looking on.

Then Conor Mac Nessa called for man after man to come forward and slay him the three, but it seemed that none of them heard him, neither Conall of the Victories nor Cethern Son of Findtan, nor Dubthach the Beetle of Ulster, nor Cuchulain himself, who was but that moment come upon the scene, until at last Owen Prince of Ferney stepped forward and took up Naisi's own sword from the ground where it lay.

'Let you strike the heads from all three of us at one blow,'

said Naisi then. 'The blade has skill enough for that; and so
we shall all be away on the same breath.' And as they stood
there side by side, and their arms bound behind them, the
Prince of Ferney shored off their three proud heads at the one
stroke. And all the Red Branch Warriors let out three heavy
shouts above them. And Deirdre broke free of the men who
held her, and she tore her bright hair and cast herself upon
the three headless bodies and cried out to them as though they
could still hear her. 'Long will be the days without you, O
sons of Usna, the days that were never wearisome in your
company. The High King of Ulster, my first betrothed, I forsook for the love of Naisi, and sorrow is to me and those that
loved me. Make keening for the heroes that were killed by
treachery at their coming back to Ulster. The sons of Usna
fell in the fight like three branches that were growing straight
and strong; their birth was beautiful and their blossoming,
and now they are cut down.

'Oh young men, digging the new grave, do not make it
narrow, leave space there for me that follow after, for I am
Deirdre without gladness, and my life at its end!'

And as they would have dragged her away from Naisi's
body, she snatched a little sharp knife from the belt of one of
the men who held her, and with a last desolate cry, drove the
blade home into her breast, and the life of her was gone from
between their hands like a bird from its broken cage.

They buried Deirdre and Naisi not far apart, at the spot
where in later times rose the great church of Armagh, and
out of her grave and out of Naisi's there grew two tall yew
trees, whose tops, when they were full grown, met above the
church roof, mingling their dark branches so that no man

might part them more. And when the sea wind hushed through the boughs, the people said, 'Listen, Deirdre and Naisi are singing together.' And when in summer the small red berries burned like jewels among the furred darkness of the boughs, they said, 'See, Deirdre and Naisi are decked for their wedding.'

10. The Hosting of Maeve

WHEN Fergus Mac Roy reached Emain Macha after the feast of Baruch, and found one of his sons dead and the other worse than dead to him, and the sons of Usna betrayed to their deaths from out of the shelter of his safe conduct, he cursed Conor the King with all the power of rage and grief within him, with all the strength of an old loyalty turned to hate, swearing to be avenged on him with fire and sword. Then he gathered his weapons and bade his charioteer to harness up, and drove like the Lord of the Wild Hunt out of Ulster, to take a new service with Maeve of Connacht.

So by King Conor's own act, the sorrow that he had tried to avert was begun indeed; for Fergus Mac Roy who had been among the greatest of the Red Branch Heroes was gone with vengeance in his heart, to join himself to Ulster's enemies. And more than one, there were, that followed him, among them Dubthach the Beetle of Ulster, and Cormac Coilinglass, the King's own son. Cuchulain did not go with them for he could not bring himself to take service with Ulster's enemies, but he went away to his own place at Dūn Dealgan, and was no more seen nor heard of at Emain Macha for a long time.

Now in Connacht it was as I told before, that the Chieftain-ship of the land passed from mother to daughter and the King counted for little. Maeve was as all the Royal women of Con-nacht had been, tall and fierce and very fair and heedful of nothing but her own wild will. And when Fergus came to her at her palace in Roscommon, she welcomed him and sought his aid in a certain matter.

For a short while before Fergus's coming, she and Ailell had had a great quarrel as to which of them had the greatest posses-sions, and in all things they had proved equal, save for the great white herd bull, the Finnbenach, who had been Maeve's, but had broken out to join the King's herd. Ailell had taunted her because the Finnbenach would not stay in the hands of a woman. This was not to be borne, and Maeve in a fury had sent for Mac Roth her steward and demanded that he should find her somewhere, anywhere in the length and breadth of Ireland, another bull as fine as the Finnbenach.

'As to finding him, that is easily done,' the steward had said, 'for the Brown Bull of Quelgney that belongs to Dara, Son of old Fachtna the Giant, is the mightiest bull in all Ireland. So broad is his back that fifty children can play upon it at the same time, and once when his keeper made him angry he trampled the man thirty feet into the ground!'

'Get him for me,' said Maeve.

But the steward shook his head. 'That is *not* so easily done, for Quelgney is deep behind the frontiers of Ulster, hard by the place where Cuchulain has his Dūn; and do you suppose, even you, great Lady, that the Ulstermen will yield up their proudest herd bull for Connacht's asking?'

And within the hour, one came running to tell her that Fergus Mac Roy stood at her gate.

Before many days and nights were past, Fergus and Maeve and Ailell were linked together with plans for a cattle raid on Ulster, Maeve because she longed for the fighting and the beautiful bright danger, to make her drunk like seven-year mead, and because she knew that if they could carry off enough cattle beside the Brown Bull himself, they would have the wealth they needed to make war on Ulster: always cattle raiding before the war; that was the way of things. Fergus because he longed for vengeance for dead sons and lost honour and broken trust. And even Ailell, because they were stronger than he.

In the first place, that all might seem well and honestly done, Maeve sent an embassy to Dara Son of Fachtna the Giant, begging the loan of the bull for one year, that he might beget sons of his own kind for the Connacht herds, and offering in exchange fifty heifers, and the friendship of Maeve, and a chariot and team worth as much as a score of women slaves.

At first Dara was tempted by so splendid an offer, but then he chanced—or maybe 'twas no chance—to hear how the men of the Connacht embassy laughed among themselves, saying how if the bull were not yielded up willingly it would be taken by force, and how in any case its task was to strengthen and enrich the Connacht herds so that the day might draw nearer when Connacht could make war on Ulster. And so when the messengers came for their answer, he said, 'An Ulster bull does best on Ulster pasture and Ulster heifers. If Queen Maeve would strengthen her herd, let her look elsewhere for her herd bull; the Pride of Ulster is not for sale.'

And when his words were brought to Maeve as she sat in her great timbered hall at Cruachan, she smiled into the fire, and said, 'So, I did not think that we should win the bull by fair means. Now we will win him by foul,' and she rose and took down a great sword from the wall and stood fingering it. 'Now the time comes to send round the Cran-Tara.'

So the black goat was sacrificed, and the hazel rod with one end dipped in its blood and the other charred in the fire was sent throughout the province of Connacht, calling the tribes together for war. And from all over Connacht the warriors and the chieftains began to gather, headed by the seven sons of Maeve, each with their own war bands; and Ket and Anluan the sons of Maga, came with three thousand men; and a host of the men of Leinster following their King who was Ailell's brother; and Ferdia came with his band, as behoved a prince of Connacht, though his heart was sore within him, remembering how he and Cuchulain had sworn the Brotherhood when they were newly men. And already in Roscommon there were Cormac Son of King Conor, and old bitter Fergus Mac Roy, and those others who had abandoned Emain Macha for the sake of Deirdre's grief and the deaths of the sons of Usna.

The weapons rang all day on the swordsmith's anvil, and all Connacht thrummed like a hornets' nest that is near to swarming, and the thunder of the chariot wheels rolled from the Shannon to the Western Sea. And Maeve went to her chief Druid and bade him look into the smoke and the sand and the entrails of the black cock still quivering with life; and tell her what he saw of the fortunes of the cattle raid. And he told her, 'Whoever else comes not back, you yourself shall come back to your hunting-runs again,' and would say no more.

But on the hill track that led back from the Druid's house to Cruachan, the chariot horses came to a rearing halt, and she saw standing at the end of the yoke pole, a maiden with broom-yellow hair hanging to her knee like a shining cloak over her green gown, and she held a gold-hilted sword with which it seemed that she was weaving in the air a web of many colours.

'Who are you that startle my horses,' cried Maeve. 'Who are you, and what is it that you do?'

'As to who I am—I am Fedelma, from the Fairy Hill of Cruachan,' said the maiden. 'As to what I do—I weave the four provinces of Ireland together for the foray into Ulster.'

'And how do you see them, the war hosts of the four provinces?' Maeve asked, against even her strong will.

'I see a whole war host stained crimson red,' said the maiden. 'A war host all blood red—blood red. And over against them I see a man, a slight man, scarce more than a boy; but the Hero light shines upon his brow. It is he that has made the war host of Maeve to be blood red . . .' She brushed the free hand she had across her eyes. 'He is like Cuchulain of Murthemney.'

Maeve cried out at the name, between fear and anger, and struck at the maiden with the goad she snatched from the hand of her charioteer—and in the flicker of the light of the eye, the maiden was not there, and the horses sprang forward along the empty hill track. And Maeve was silent, very silent, as she drove.

The humming and the drumming and all the bronze clan-gour of Connacht making ready for war, came to Ulster like 'twere the distant thunder of doom among the hills. And doom indeed seemed in the note of it, for many years before, a woman of the Lordly Ones, married to a mortal farmer, had been forced by certain of the Ulster Nobles to run a race against the King's chariot horses. She had won her race, but had fallen at the winning post, and with her death upon her, she had cursed the men of Ulster. 'From this day forward, the sorrow that you have put on me, let it fall on you; and at the time you are most needing your strength, with the enemy hard upon you, the weakness of a dying woman shall come upon the warriors of Ulster.' And as she cursed them, so it had been ever since. And now Conor the King himself lay at Emain Macha, and his son Cuscrid, and Owen Prince of Ferney and even Conall of the Victories lay moaning on their beds with not so much strength in them as would serve to lift a spear. All the Red Branch Warriors save one; Cuchulain was of Ulster only on his mother's side, and his father's blood in him, the blood of the Sun Lord himself, was stronger than any curse.

Now Cuchulain was at Ard Cuillen on the southern borders of Murthemney settling some dispute between two of his chieftains, when the Great Weakness struck, and he heard the deep war thunder of the four provinces of Ireland gathering to the south, and he knew what was afoot. And that same evening as he sat at supper in the hall of one of the chieftains, waited on by the sorely troubled women, while the men sprawled groaning on the sleeping-benches, a light war spear was flung in at the open door and when he plucked it up, he saw cut on the shaft certain word-signs in the Ogham script. 'Take this spear with the love of thy friend and all but foster father, Fergus Mac Roy. They say that there will be a spear-dance in the Gap of the North, within two days.'

Then Cuchulain looked into the eyes of Laeg the Charioteer, who being no Ulsterman by birth, was also free of the curse of the Ulster warriors. 'This is from Fergus Mac Roy, to give me warning. The hosts of Ireland will be in the Gap of the North within two days.'

'Then the time comes to be yoking the chariot,' Laeg said.

'First the time comes to send the warning back into Ulster. At Emain Macha they may be safe, but with the Great Weakness upon them, it is little good that the scattered warriors will do by biding in the open country to be slain like oxen. They must make for Emain, or take to the woods and glens where the host of Ireland will not find them. You've a busy night before you, Laeg my friend, but the young and swift among the women will help you. Once you set the word going it will run like heath fire, and when it is running, then come back to me here and yoke the chariot and set the war-blades to the wheel hubs.'

'And you?' said Laeg.

'I have a thing to do that will maybe gain us a night and a day for our warriors to be clear of the open country before the spear dance starts.'

And while Laeg gathered up the boys and young women of the place and set about the task of warning Ulster, he went to the stable where the Black Seinglend and the Grey of Macha were trampling and snorting as though they already smelled battle on the wind, and taking a pony mare of the chieftain's renowned for her speed, rode off to the valley woods far below, where a small white-running stream through the brown autumn bracken and squat wind-shaped oak trees marked the boundary of Murthemney. And there he cut an oak sapling and twisted it into a garland such as men use for target practice, and cut on the strong central stem a certain message in Ogham, and hung it over the pillar stone of Ard Cuillen beside the stream bank.

At dusk the next evening the host of Maeve came to the pillar stone of Ard Cuillen and found the oak garland upon it, and read there Cuchulain's name and the warning that they should not pass the pillar stone that night, for if they did, he would take a mighty revenge on them at the next day's sunrise.

Then Maeve said, 'A pity it would be that first blood should go to Ulster, for there are those among the war host who would call it an ill omen, and lose all heart within them.' And though she bit her nails in her fury, until the crimson started at the quick, she knew that there was nothing to be done but to make camp for that night and advance no farther into Ulster until morning.

The first snow of the winter fell that night, and the men could find no shelter nor place to cook their food, while the chariot ponies stood shivering miserably with their heads down and their rumps to the whirling whiteness. But at dawn the snow ceased and the skies cleared, and the sun broke through. And the bone-chilled war host raised a yell and ran to harness up the chariots.

'Ach well, it has gained us one night,' Cuchulain said to his charioteer, when from the Dūn of Ard Cuillen he heard the distant thunder of the war host flowing into Murthemney. And he laid an arm across the other's shoulders, laughing. 'And the snow shall stand friend to us and traitor to them like the fine brave Ulster snow it is! Harness up, my brother.'

And so before the sun was past the blue shoulder of Slieve Fuad, Cuchulain in his war chariot came swooping down on the track of the host, where all the snow of the broad glen was trampled and mazed with tracks of men and horses and the ruts of the chariot wheels, and swept to and fro across it like a hound nosing out a trail, until the traces had told him all that they had to tell.

'More than five thousand men have passed this way. Surely this is a cattle raid beyond any that ever was known before,' Cuchulain said, 'and they were travelling fast as lash and goad can drive. Now, that is a thing that we can alter a little, at all events,' and he laughed and took the goad and the reins from Laeg and sent the team bounding forward. He swung them wide of the war host, touching them about the haunches with the goad now on this side and now on that like a gadfly, yet never so as to draw blood. 'On, my beauties, my brothers! This is a race worth the winning!'

And a while beyond noon, with the race truly won, he came sweeping in far beyond the advance guard of Maeve's host, and turned to meet them. He gave back goad and reins to Laeg, for from now on it would be for Laeg to drive and for him to fight the chariot; and as he waited, listening, Laeg holding the sweating team in check, he felt all Ulster at his back, beyond the wild glens of Bregia, and knew that until the Great Weakness passed from his comrades, it was for him to hold the passes against the whole war host of Ireland; and he sent up in his heart a great cry to Lugh of the Shining Spear: 'Father, if I am indeed your son, help me in this, for sorely I will be needing your help—you who gave me as a gift to Ulster, let me be a gift worth the having! Let my horses trample the enemy beneath their hooves as rotten apples at the cider harvest, and let the slaying of my spear be like lightning blasting them through and through!'

The sound of hooves and chariot wheels stole upon the autumn quietness of the glens that was full of the trickle of snow water and the soughing of the little wind, and two light chariots came sweeping over the shoulder of the moors, down towards the ford that just there crossed the river. 'Queen Maeve sends her scouts ahead like a prudent war leader,' Cuchulain said softly, when he saw them. 'Well, they shall tell one thing to their mistress at least—that the passes into Ulster do not lie open to all comers! Now Laeg! They are across the ford—make for the nearest of them!'

They raced down upon the first of the scouting chariots, and as they thundered yelling past, Cuchulain leaned out over the rim and with one mighty sword stroke smote the heads of both warrior and driver from their shoulders. Then almost without orders the Black Seinglend and the Grey of Macha swung round upon the other chariot as the driver lashed his horses to meet them, and again Cuchulain's sword flashed in the snow-paled sunlight, and again two heads fell.

Then Cuchulain leapt from the chariot and cut the traces of the terrified Irish horses and let them run, and himself he turned to the alder scrub along the river, and found a young tree with four branches, and cut it down and lopped the branches and trimmed what remained into sharp points. And on each of the four prongs he impaled one head of those that he had struck off, and he set the pole up at the river ford for a warning. And that place was called Athgowla, the Ford of the Forked Pole, ever after.

And when, a while later, Maeve and her war host came roaring down to the ford, they found the bloody heads on their forked pole, like a tree of death bearing hideous fruits, and knew, if they had not known it before, that Cuchulain held the passes. But though they sent out the best hunters among them and scoured the glens of Slieve Fuad and Slieve Cuillen, not a hide nor hair could they find of the Hound of Ulster among his own hills.

Nevertheless the war host poured on, fanning out like a forest fire and spreading great bursts of black ruin and desolation through the lands of Bregia and Murthemney. Many a farmsteading went up in flames, many a shrieking woman was carried off into slavery in the days that followed, while the snow melted and the early winter was turning green again. But the war host did not go scaithless, for slingstones whistled through their camps at night, and by day Cuchulain hung about their flanks, cutting off stragglers, slaying by ones and twos at first, then as his battle frenzy grew upon him, descending upon the whole war host to slay as a reaper cuts his long swaithe through standing barley. Scores and then hundreds at a time went down before his onslaught, cut down by whistling spear and whirling war scythes, and trampled into red ruin under the thundering wheels and the thundering hooves of the team.

And now for the first time, the hosts of Connacht and Leinster and the rest saw the man who had played wolf-pack unseen on their flanks, the Hound of Ulster, and saw him in the full terror of his battle frenzy, the Hero light blazing upon his brow and the jet of black blood shooting skyward to make that murk like a rushing storm-cloud that hung above his head. And indeed now it was not only with weapons that he killed, for at the very sight of him rushing towards them behind his flying team, it is told how once a whole company of Maeve's warriors fell dead from sheer horror at the aspect of him.

Maeve began to grow desperate, and sent message after message to him under cover of the Truce Branch, striving to buy him over with promises of greater power and wealth than ever man held in Ulster. But Cuchulain laughed in the faces of the envoys, and called up his charioteer again for a new foray. But matters could not long endure in such a way; and on the fourth day Maeve and Cuchulain stood facing each other across a narrow glen that was like a sword gash full of shadows in the hills that rose towards Slieve Cuillen, Maeve with her chiefs and captains behind her, her spear in her hand and the Royal Gold on her head and her long pale hair streaming sideways in the buffeting autumn wind; Cuchulain like a dark flame in his war gear, his black hair flying like hers from under his war-cap, and no man with him save Laeg, at all. And Maeve marvelled in her heart that this slight dark stripling—for indeed he looked little more—should be the terror of her whole war host, who, in his battle frenzy, was like a red War God rather than a warrior. But she had not called this meeting between them to see what like he was.

And to and fro across the narrow glen, the green plover calling on the slopes behind them, they called to each other, offering and refusing terms, bargaining and counter bargaining. At last and at last, leaning on his spear, Cuchulain called across the glen, 'All day we have argued this thing, and I am very weary. Here then is my last word, O Queen of Connacht; listen to it well, for there is no more to come after; and on these terms and these alone, I will cease to harry the war host. But an hour's trail northward of this place, midway into the Gap of Ulster, there is a river ford. There I will take my stand, and you shall send against me your champions, one champion at a time, and one each day. And to each one I will give fight in defence of the ford. And while each combat lasts, so long may the war hosts of Ireland press forward into Ulster; but when each battle ends, the host shall halt, wherever it be, and camp until the next morning. These are my terms, Maeve of Connacht; think well before you refuse them.'

Maeve thought for a long while, leaning also on her spear. Then she lifted her head and shouted back across the glen.

'Better to advance a spear's throw a day, than to advance not at all. And better to lose one man a day than a hundred. So be it then, Cuchulain, Hound of Ulster, I agree to your terms.'

11. The Fight at the Ford

So Cuchulain took his stand at the ford, and that same evening, Maeve sent against him the first of her champions, and they fought knee-deep in the shallows of the ford. But the fore-guard of the Irish host had not moved a bowshot from their last night's camp before their champion went down with Cuchulain's spear through his heart, and they must needs camp again for that night. But Cuchulain kept his word and they slept unmolested through the darkness. And the next day Maeve sent her second champion into battle, and that time the rest of the war host moved up and all of them were three spear throws farther north when the second combat ended as the first had done.

Champion after champion came, and each one Cuchulain met and slew, and each time the war hosts of Ireland advanced while the fight lasted, and halted and made camp for the night when the fighting was ended. At last the Queen chose to send Fergus Mac Roy himself against the Holder of the Ford; and when Cuchulain saw who it was that came against him a shock of cold fell upon his heart. But there was a thing in his foster father's face, a flicker that was like laughter under the brown beard; and when they came together in the midst of the ford, Fergus whispered to him across the shield rim, 'Will you run now, little fighting cock, if I do the same for you on another day?' And the laughter leapt from Fergus into Cuchulain's heart.

'Surely, that is a fair bargain—but as it is yours to choose the time now, it shall be mine to choose the other time, when it is your turn to run.'

Then they struck at each other fierce and swift above the bronze shield rims, so that those looking on would think that they fought to the death indeed; and in a while Cuchulain allowed Fergus to strike the broad spear from his hand, and sprang back with a cry, and turned and ran.

Then all the war host of Maeve shouted and drummed spear on shield until it seemed that the very glens of Slieve Cuillen and Slieve Fuad rang with their scornful mirth. But nevertheless, the fight was over for that day, as Fergus reminded them, and himself swaggered back to stand beside the Queen's chariot; and they made camp for another night, and in the morning sent yet another champion to the ford.

But Maeve, furious that one man should so hold up her whole war host, had made a plan; and so while this day's fighting was going on—and it lasted long, for she had chosen for it one of the greatest of all the Connacht champions, Natchrantal—she gathered a war band of picked warriors, and leaving the rest of the war host to keep the bargain, drove headlong into Ulster like any wild cattle raider that ever was since the world began. And with none to hinder them, for Cuchulain had his hands full at the ford, and the men of Ulster still lay as though tranced in their weakness, they cut through into Armagh, burning and plundering as they went, until they came into the northern glens of Slieve Cuillen, and found the Brown Bull sheltering there with his herd of fifty favourite cows; and they drove him off in triumph, trampling and thundering his fury in their midst.

Now Cuchulain, having made an end of that day's fight, was ranging the countryside in search of game, for Maeve's army had all Ireland behind to feed them, but he and Laeg must hunt for themselves. And he beheld the Brown Bull in the midst of his captors, and rushed to the rescue, but though he slew many of the cattle raiders, among them their leader, Banblai Son of Buic, yet he could not bring off the Brown Bull, and with sick rage burning in his heart, must see the pride and the lord of the Ulster herds driven south into Connacht, while he was bound to the ford which at all costs he must defend— for he knew well enough that the fighting would not end with the capture of the Brown Bull that was the first reason for it. To dishonour the province of Ulster would not be enough now that the war host had tasted the wild-honey taste of plunder. And so it proved as the days went by.

Indeed now that she had broken her sworn bargain once, it seemed to Maeve that she might just as well cast it off altogether, and she began to loose her champions against Cuchulain no longer singly but sometimes in bands of ten or twenty at a time, so that he was sore beset and had wounds as well as weariness to drain his strength. And then a new danger came upon him, for one night as he lay too tired to sleep beside the little fire that Laeg had made for him, a woman came out of the dark into the firelight beside the chariot wheel. A woman young and good to look upon, with red hair and arched red eyebrows and a gown and mantle wrapped about her that were red as blood; and she bent over Cuchulain until her darkly glowing hair swept across his mouth, and let her eyes smile into his.

Cuchulain started to his elbow. 'Who are you? If you come from the camp of Maeve of Connacht, let you go back there with whatever you have spied out to tell her.'

'That is no courteous way to be speaking to a King's daughter,' said the woman.

'What King would that be?'

'The King of a very far country whose name you would not know. But even there we have heard of the Hound of Ulster and his mighty deeds. Therefore, I come, because I would see for myself, and now that I have seen—it is in my heart that here with the Hound of Ulster I will stay.'

Her voice was low and clear as the note of a small bronze bell, and her hands that were on his pleaded also; but Cuchulain shook her off.

'I am worn out with fighting. There is no mind in me to be having aught to do with women.'

The woman sprang back and stood looking down at him. 'It shall go hard with you, then,' said she, 'when next you have to do with men; for come tomorrow's fighting, I shall be as an eel about your feet in the bottom of the ford.'

And suddenly between flicker and flutter of the firelight she was no longer there. Only a great black crow sat on the rim of the chariot above him, then rose with a derisive *kaak*, and flapped away. And he knew that he had been speaking with the Morrigan, the Lady of War herself. But Laeg still sat with his spear across his knees, blinking into the fire. Only the horses tethered nearby shifted uneasily, and almost it might have been a dream.

Yet when Cuchulain rose next morning and called Laeg to help him with his war gear, and went out yet again to defend the ford, there was a heaviness on him and a sense of dread that he had never known before. And hardly had he joined combat with Loch Son of Mofobis who was that day's chosen champion, than a white heifer with red ears came plunging down the bank and thrust against his side, hampering his sword arm and driving up the sheets of spray to blind him, and Cuchulain snatched free a light throwing spear and flung it, catching her in the eye, and with a woman's shriek she ceased to be. But in the same instant the coils of a great black eel were weaving and flowing and tightening around his feet, and while he staggered half off balance and striving to tear free, he lowered his shield a moment, and Loch's spear caught him in the shoulder, and the eel was gone and in its place a great grey she-wolf with one eye sprang from the water at his throat. And as he staggered back, turning his spear against her, Loch struck in under his guard and wounded him in the flank. At that his battle fury rose, so that flinging off the she-wolf, who was gone like a curl of smoke, he leapt high in the air and drove his spear over Loch's shield rim and deep into his breast, and split his heart in two.

Loch gave a shuddering cry and crashed down to his knees, yet clung there to his spear butt to keep from falling farther. 'Let me up,' he gasped, and the breath rattled in his throat. 'Let me up, Hound of Ulster, that I may fall with my face to your side of the ford, not backward as one defeated, towards the war hosts of my own people!'

'That is a warrior's boon you ask,' said Cuchulain, strangely gentle. 'And gladly I grant it to you,' and he stooped and set his arm about Loch Son of Mofobis, and aided him to rise and gain the farther bank and there Loch fell dead, with his face towards Ulster.

With the death of Loch, a great weariness and sorrow fell upon Cuchulain, so that it was as though the shadow of black wings hung between him and the sun, for he was weak with many wounds, and worn out with long fighting, and had slain men who he would fain have had for friends. And he had not slept for many nights, save leaning on his spear, and he knew that the time was coming when his heart and strength must fail.

On the second evening after Loch's death, Cuchulain stood leaning against the chariot bow while Laeg tended his wounds, and looked out towards the hosts of Ireland that by now had all but reached the ford. 'Surely behind us there must be *some* beginning to stir from their weakness,' he said. 'Do you start northward at first light, take the first horse you find on your way, and make for Emain Macha. Rouse me out whatever of men you can, even the merest war-knot, for the time is coming when I can no longer hold the marches of Ulster alone.'

'My heart is sore to leave you here,' Laeg said, 'but if the voice of one man can rouse Ulster, then Ulster shall rouse and come to your aid.'

And when the morning came, he set off for Emain Macha, while Cuchulain, suddenly more alone than ever in his life before, turned back to face the war hosts of Maeve. That evening he made his own fire, and lay down with his cloak about him as he had lain so many nights, at the foot of an ancient grave mound where there was shelter from the bitter wind that was stripping the last blackened leaves from the alder trees. But he missed sorely the soft whistling of Laeg as he made ready the evening food, and desolation wrapped him round so that for very weariness he could have laid his head on his arm and wept like an unhappy girl-child of seven summers.

For a while he lay watching the camp fires of Munster and Connacht across the river, so many and many camp fires, and his own small fire solitary like himself at the foot of Da Derga's grave mound. And as he watched, he saw a man walking through the great camp, lit and lost and lit again by the watch fires, and no man stirring nor turning to look as he went by. His tunic shimmered with goldwork and his speckled green cloak was fastened with a brooch like a silver targe. On one arm he carried a black shield bordered and studded with silver, and in his right hand, two spears. He came straight down to the ford and crossed over, his feet as light and sure on the water as they had been another time on the bog cotton grass.

And watching him come, Cuchulain remembered suddenly where he had seen the man before.

The stranger came and bent over him, his face sternly kind in the firelight whose radiance seemed to blur and blend with his own. 'A hard fight you have fought, my Hound, and there is more fighting yet to do. You are weary and stiff with wounds and have not slept for many nights. Sleep now, Cuchulain my son; three days and three nights you shall sleep, as quiet as Chieftain Derga in his grave mound.'

'And who will hold the ford?'

'I will hold the ford, and no one shall know that it is not yourself that holds it.'

And Cuchulain knew, as though it were a thing he had always known, that Lugh his father had come to stand with him in his sorest need. Then he fell into a sleep as deep as the bottom of Lough Ney and as dark and soft as the fur of the black beavers that build there; and never knew when Lugh the Sun Lord laid healing herbs to his wounds, nor when, at next day's sunrise, he took up Cuchulain's weapons, and with them Cuchulain's whole aspect so that no mortal man could have guessed that he was not indeed the Hound of Ulster, and strode down to the ford.

And still the men of Ulster lay helpless, from the King in Emain Macha to the youngest spear-bearer at his gate, for all that Laeg could do to rouse them. But in the Boys' House life was as usual, for the Great Weakness fell only upon grown men; and when the boys in training heard from Laeg how sorely it went with Cuchulain their hero (and there were some there still, on the verge of Taking Valour, who remembered Cuchulain as the Leader of the Boys' House when first they came to it), they caught up their weapons, and some took the chariots and horses from the stables, and with Follaman the King's youngest son for their captain, they marched out to meet the war hosts of Ireland, for the honour of Ulster and the aiding of the Hound. And beside the King's tall weapon-hacked pillar stone, they swore that they would not return to Emain Macha without Ailell's crown for a trophy.

They came up with the enemy, and three times they charged them, yelling their war-cry; and at each charge three times their number fell before them; but at each charge there were fewer left of the Boys' Band, until they dwindled to a mere valiant handful, storming forward at their young captain's heels, flinging themselves upon the enemy spears, until the last went down under the hooves of the chariot teams. And so they kept their faith with Cuchulain and their vow at the King's pillar stone, and since they could not bring back the crown of Ailell hanging on their spears, they came never back to Emain Macha at all, and the women who wept for them were their mothers.

All this came to pass while Cuchulain lay in his tranced sleep; and when he woke, feeling well and strong as though the morning were the morning of the world, he saw the boys' bodies scattered through the Gap of the North, and all across the battle ground, and understood what had passed.

Then a great rage rose in him, a high wind of rage that beat blood red before his eyes. And he cried aloud to the morning emptiness, 'Nobly you have kept faith with me, young brothers! So now will I keep faith with you!' and he armed himself and harnessed Black Seinglend and the Grey of Macha who still grazed near by. For this time there would be no waiting at the ford for the enemy to come to him. That was over. And as he worked, quietly and unhurriedly, talking to the horses as he led each up beside the hollywood yoke-pole, and secured the swinging harness, encouraging and making much of them as a good charioteer should do, the red haze beat and beat and beat behind his eyes, and in his ears the blood was like the pounding of the wolfskin war drums that the Dark People make in the hills in the time of sacrifice.

When all was ready he leapt into the chariot, and with a yell headed straight for the war host of Maeve, sending up great wings of water on either side as he thundered across the ford, and as he went, feet wide planted on the lurching chariot floor, knotting the reins about and about his waist, that he might have both hands free. And with that yell, the battle frenzy that until that moment he had kept leashed and muzzled, burst free and leapt up in him, and the Hero light flared upon his forehead, and as the horrified men of Ireland sprang for their weapons, it seemed to them that some fiend hooded with fire and driving the flying steeds of Hell, came thundering down upon them, sweeping with him the spread wings of a black and mighty tempest to engulf them all.

Cuchulain did not charge straight upon the war host, but yelling, howling, singing to his flying team, he thundered about and about and about the host, until the shrieking chariot wheels that spurted fire at every flint in the way, ploughed the earth to ruts like the ditches of a mighty camp; and the dartings of his great spear were bright and blasting strokes of the lightning flash that slew all before it; and the curved war-blades on the chariot wheels caught and mangled and mowed down the enemy until bodies were piled upon bodies for a fortress wall within the ditches of the camp. And with Cuchulain went a wild and screaming wind and darkness that was full of terror and flying things, and as he yelled in his wrath, every demon and night-thing in all Ireland shrieked and howled in answer.

And as terror of the Unseen in the war host mounted upon the terror of the Hound of Ulster, men swayed and surged together, each one hampering his comrade's spear arm, and some fell by each other's weapons and others were trampled to death or crushed by the terrified chariot steeds loose in their midst, and some fell dead from fear alone, as a man choking in the grip of a hideous dream. And only when day had worn away to first starlight, and the horses of his team were quenched and weary, Cuchulain drew them off and returned to his own place.

Close on two hundred chiefs and princes of the hosts of Maeve died that day, and lesser warriors and horses and warhounds and women without number.

And this was called ever after 'The Slaughter of Murthemney'; the slaughter that Cuchulain made in vengeance for the death of the Boys' Band.

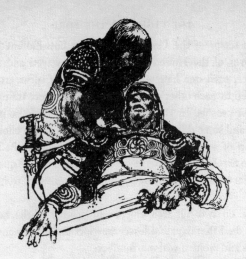

12. The Death of Ferdia

THAT night Maeve called a council among those that were yet living of her chiefs and princes, and they determined to loose upon Cuchulain the terrible Clan Calatin.

Now the Clan Calatin was a wizard of great and dreadful power, and he and his twenty-seven sons formed one being, so that each son was as it were a limb of the father, in the way that elm suckers are still part of the tree they spring from; a whole war band sharing one mind and one heart. So venomous they were that any weapon they handled would kill within nine days if it so much as broke the skin.

And so next morning as Cuchulain turned away from tending the horses—he had lain down to sleep in full war gear as usual —he saw this ghastly monster trotting towards the ford, a spear in every right hand.

Cuchulain caught up his own spear and ran, and the monster, seeing him, quickened to a run also, seeming to flow many-legged along the ground like a pack of hounds. And so both came racing down to meet at the ford, and as they neared, Clan Calatin checked an instant and flung at the Ulster champion its whole flight of venomed spears.

While the flight was yet in the air, Cuchulain flung his own spear in return, and all twenty-eight of the monster's barbs he caught on his shield so that not one of them would draw a single drop of blood. But with the weight of the shafts dragging down on the great bullshide buckler it was quite unmanage-able, and as he snatched his sword from its sheath to hack them away, the monster sprang at him, swifter than any mortal flesh and blood could strike, and seizing him in a grip that had the strength of eight and twenty men, flung him down, and snarl-ing and slavering, ground his face into the sharp river-washed gravel at the ford's edge.

A great hoarse shout broke from Cuchulain's strained and tortured heart, and the sound of it came like a cry for aid to one of the Ulster men who had followed Fergus Mac Roy. Fiacha Son of Firaba had drawn close to watch the fight, and suddenly he felt the old loyalties of the Red Branch rise within him, and he drew his sword and sprang in to Cuchulain's aid, and with one mighty blow struck off six and fifty claw-hands of Clan Calatin that were grinding his face into the murderous gravel.

Then Cuchulain leapt up, his face a streaming mask of blood, and with his own sword which had been prisoned under him, struck off the shrieking and snarling heads of the monster, and hacked it limb from limb that nothing might be left to tell Maeve of Fiacha's part in the deed. 'For it were poor thanks to a friend in time of need, that he and all his following should suffer death for it,' he said.

That was the last fight but one of Cuchulain at the ford, and the last fight was the sorest one to him of all.

He knew in his own heart how it must be, and when that same night Laeg returned to him, he said, 'Ach well, maybe I can finish the task without the men of Ulster. Now that the Clan Calatin is dead, I have fought and overcome all the greatest of Maeve's warriors save one.'

'And that one?'

'Ferdia Mac Daman—after old Fergus, the greatest of them all,' said Cuchulain, and he turned from his charioteer to the rough trunk of the alder tree against which he leaned, and hid his face in the crook of his arm.

And that same night, over in the camp of Maeve, which by now had crossed the river farther up into the hills where the rocks broke it, over in the camp of the joined war hosts of Ireland, when the evening meal was done—they had eaten well, of Murthemney's fattest cattle—Maeve sent for Ferdia Son of Daman to come to her beside her own fire. And he went with a heavy heart, knowing all too well what the summons meant.

Seated on her piled crimson chariot cushions. Maeve leaned back against the wheel of her chariot and looked up at him with the firelight in her pale hair and pale bright eyes, as though even she were not sure how to break in to the things that she would speak of.

'Ferdia Mac Daman,' she said at last, 'I know how it is between you and this Hound of Ulster, and therefore, all this while I have not asked that you should go down against him in this long duel of champions. But you are the last left among the *great* warriors, and now it is you that must take your weapons and your turn.'

'So, you know how it is between me and the Hound of

Ulster,' Ferdia said, standing before her. 'You know then that I will not do as you bid me in this thing.'

'Have you forgotten that you are a man of Connacht and I am Connacht's Queen?'

'I have not forgotten, but I will not go down weapon in hand against my friend.'

'We are all the friends you have,' said the Queen.

'My brother, then,' Ferdia said, his blue eyes levelled like a spear into her pale ones.

Maeve the Queen leaned forward. 'I can give you sweeter than a brother.'

'And what would that be?'

'Does not Findabair my daughter seem to you fair? Take your weapons and go down against Cuchulain, and if you prevail, then you shall take Findabair of the Fair Eyebrows for your wife.'

Ferdia knew well enough what she offered, for to wed the Royal Daughter was to be King of Connacht when her time came to be Queen. 'And be one day as great and powerful as Ailell? You are gracious, my Queen, but I've no wishes that way.'

There was a long silence, and the night wind played with the flames and the horses stamped in the picket lines. And Maeve's eyes narrowed like those of a wild cat's before it spits, and like a cat's, too, they seemed to shine of themselves in the firelight. 'So be it, then, since neither gifts of friendship nor your loyalty to Connacht can move you,' she said, 'let you think of this, Ferdia Mac Daman: you alone of all the warriors of Ireland have refused to go out against the Hound at my asking. You say it is because he is your friend—ach now, a fine and noble-sounding reason—but who's to say it is the true one? Who's to say the true reason is not that you are afraid?'

'My comrades of the war host know me better than that,' Ferdia said.

'The war host? Even those that lie dead now by the ford, because the honour of Connacht was more dear to them than life? In Tir-Nan-Og, in the Islands of the West, will they not say that Ferdia Mac Daman betrayed and deserted them? Will that not make a fine song for all the harpers of Ireland to sing at every chieftain's hearth? You will not have the Queen's daughter for your wife, but after this, what woman is there that will mate with *you*? What man will share the drinking horn with you, Ferdia Mac Daman who forsook his own people in their time of need?'

Ferdia stood while a man's heart might beat seven times, staring across the fire at her, white as a ghost already, to the very lips. Then he turned and strode away in grief and bitter anger, to find his charioteer. 'Have the team harnessed and all things ready by first light,' he said. 'We drive to the ford.'

The news ran through the camp like a thin whispering mid-winter wind, and Ferdia's own men were sick at heart, knowing that their lord would never in this world come driving back from Cuchulain's ford.

The world still slept in shadow though the sky already rang with light, when Ferdia came to the ford, and finding no sign yet of Cuchulain, lay down on the cushions and skin rugs from the chariot, and slept the light ear-cocked sleep of the hunter until he should come.

It was full daylight when he woke to hear his charioteer calling him, and the nearing thunder of a war chariot that he knew for Cuchulain's even before he looked.

Cuchulain came whirling down to the ford in a smother of dust and sprang from the chariot while the tall red-haired driver wheeled the team aside. And one on each bank of the river they stood and looked across to the other. 'So you have come at last, Ferdia who I have called my brother,' Cuchulain said sadly. 'Every day I have wondered, but in my heart I believed you would not come.'

'Why should I not come? Am I not a man of Connacht like the others?' Ferdia shouted back with a wild defiance.

'Aye—and yet when we were with Skatha and learned the warriors' arts, were we not shoulder to shoulder in every fight? Did we not hunt together the same trails, and feast together and share the drink cup and the sleeping-place when the day was over?'

Ferdia sounded as though he sobbed. 'You speak of our friendship, but all that is best forgotten. It shall not avail you now, Hound of Ulster, it shall not avail you now!'

Cuchulain made a gesture with his free arm that was strangely like to that of a bird with a broken wing. 'So be it, it is forgotten. What weapons shall we use?'

'We used to have something of skill with the light throw-spears,' Ferdia said.

So each champion called to his driver to bring the javelins from his chariot, and all the first half of that day, standing one at each end of the ford, they sent the light throw-spears humming to and fro like darting dragon-flies across the water. But each was as skilled at catching the missiles on his shield as he was at casting them; and by noon, neither had drawn blood. Then they turned to the heavier bronze-tipped throw-spears, and by evening both had their wounds to show, but neither more than the other. And when the dusk under the alder trees grew too deep for clear aim, they broke off as by common consent, and tossed their weapons to the waiting charioteers.

'That is over for one day,' Cuchulain said.

And they went to meet each other in the midst of the ford

and flung their arms about each other's shoulders. Then they both returned together to the Ulster bank. And that night the two champions washed each other's hurts and shared their food and spread their sleeping-rugs together between the two chariots, while their horses cropped together at the thin wintry grass and their drivers warmed themselves at the same fire.

At dawn they rose, ate a little bannock and cheese, and then went down again to the ford. And that day Cuchulain had the choice of weapons, and all the daylight hours they fought from the chariots with the great broad-bladed spears for close combat and at sunset when the last wintry light glimmered up from the water, and the drivers and the horses were spent and staggering, and both champions were gashed and bloody as battle-torn boars, they flung aside their reeking spears and sprang down into the shallows to embrace each other; and that night all was as it had been the night before, and Cuchulain and Ferdia slept as they had done when they were boys, under the same rug.

The next morning as they took up their shields, Cuchulain burst out, gripping the other's shoulder, 'Ferdia, Ferdia, how could you come against me for the sake of a woman—and a woman who has been offered to half the champions of the host —even to me, if I would yield up the ford for her sake.'

'For the Royal Daughter of Connacht?' Ferdia said bitterly. 'Never think it. I should have been shamed through Roscommon, through the whole of Connacht, if I had not come down to the ford. *She* would have made sure as to that, Maeve the Queen!'

'And so for your own honour, you would slay me,' Cuchulain said, the voice of him heavy with grief.

And Ferdia raised his head and looked at him without a

word. But it was as though he said, 'It was not *I* that was champion of all Skatha's boys.'

'The choice of weapons is yours,' Cuchulain said.

And that day, all the wintry daylight hours, they fought in midstream with their heavy leaf-bladed iron swords, and though they wounded each other sorely again and again, still neither gained any advantage. But that night when the first fierce stars of Orion shone frost bright through the alder branches, the champions slept apart, and their horses grazed on different pastures and their charioteers warmed themselves at separate fires.

In the next dawn, when Ferdia rose, he knew that this would be the last day's fighting, and he knew very surely what the end of it would be. He armed himself with especial care, and over his striped silken tunic and leather loinguard he bound a great flat stone across his belly, and over that an iron apron, for he knew that Cuchulain would use the Gae Bolg today. He put on his crested war-helm rich with enamelling; and belted on his sword and took up his bullshide buckler with the fifty bronze bosses. Then he went down to the ford and crossed over to his own side. And waiting there, with a sudden wild defiant gaiety, he fell to tossing up his mighty spears and catching them again, idly, like a juggler playing with apples.

And on his own side of the ford, Cuchulain the Hound of Ulster stood watching, then said over his shoulder to Laeg his charioteer, 'Laeg, will you do a thing for me? If I give ground today, do you give me your scorn to spur me on. Mock at me and burn me up with shame,' and even as he said it, he thought how Ferdia had done that thing for him when first he strove to cross the Bridge of Leaps, and he could have wept like a woman.

Then he called across the river. 'What weapons shall it be today?'

'Today the choice is yours,' said Ferdia.

'Then let it be all or any,' Cuchulain said.

And all that morning until the sun stood at noon, they fought with the spears, yet neither could overcome the other. Then Cuchulain drew his sword and set on with that, striving to strike in over Ferdia's guard. Three times he leapt in the air to drive the deadly blade down over the rim of Ferdia's buckler, but each time Ferdia caught him on the broad face of the shield itself, and flung him off into the deep water beside the ford; and Laeg cried out, fiercely mocking, 'See now! He casts you off as the river casts a rotten stick, he grinds you as the quern stone grinds a grain of barley! Little manikin, never call yourself a warrior, lest the women of Ulster should make themselves sick with laughing!'

And at the sound of Laeg's mockery, at last Cuchulain's battle frenzy came upon him, and he seemed all at once taller than tall Ferdia, and the Hero light blazed about his head, and springing in upon each other the two champions were locked together, reeling and trampling to and fro, while the demons and banshees and all unearthly things of the glens whirled and shrieked about their leaping blades, and the very waters of the river took fright and rolled and boiled back from the ford, so that for a while and a while they fought on dry land.

Presently Cuchulain stumbled on a shifting stone, and in the moment that he was off guard, Ferdia drove in his sword and wounded him in the shoulder so that the blood splashed down on to the stones of the ford, and the river ran skeined with scarlet; and as though the sight of the blood maddened him, he began to press upon Cuchulain, striking and thrusting like some great fair-haired fiend of battle, until at last Cuchulain could bear it no more and shouted to Laeg to throw him the Gae Bolg.

Ferdia whipped down his shield to guard his loins and belly, but even as he did so, Cuchulain had caught the dreadful spear as Laeg flung it to him, and leapt and thrust it downward over Ferdia's guard so that it split asunder the flat stone and pierced through Ferdia's armour, and plunged in between belly and breast, deep into his body, so that it burst his great heart, and his life came pouring out.

'It is finished,' cried Ferdia. 'Grief upon me! I have my death at your hand, Cuchulain my brother, and to you is the victory!'

Cuchulain caught him as he fell, and carried him to the bank —to the Ulster bank, that he might not die on the hated Connacht shore—and laid him down. And then with a roaring as of many seas in his ears and a blackness before his eyes, sank forward across the body of his friend, with his arms still about him.

Laeg stooped and tried desperately to rouse him. 'Up! Up Cuchulain! The hosts of Ireland will be upon us now that their last champion is dead!'

'Why should I rise again? I have killed my brother,' Cuchulain said, and the darkness closed over him, so that he never heard the thunder of hooves nor the shouted triumph of the war songs as the hosts of Queen Maeve poured through the glens into Ulster. Nor did he know when Laeg lifted him into the chariot and goaded the team into a racing gallop for the refuge of Sleive Fuad's northern glens.

13. The End of the Cattle Raid

'The men of Ulster are being slain and the women carried away and the cattle driven, and Cuchulain alone holds the Gap of the North against the four Provinces of Ireland!' Laeg had cried through Emain Macha; but it had seemed that the stupefied warriors scarcely heard him; only some wagged their heads a little, as though he had cried that the geese were in the kale plot.

But when in despair he had snatched a fresh horse from the Red Branch stables and gone flying back to rejoin his lord, the women took up his cry: 'Do you not hear? Rouse up! Conor Mac Nessa, if ever you were a fighting man before this sickness came upon you, rouse up and rouse your warriors and go to aid Cuchulain! Do you not understand that the war hosts of all Ireland are at the gates of Ulster, and none but the Hound of Ulster to stand alone in the gate?'

And slowly, as the Curse of Macha started to wear thin, the words of the women began to pierce through to the dazed minds of the warriors, and their eyes, which had been empty or full of clouds, began again to be the eyes of the Red Branch Heroes that their women and their enemies knew. And at last Conor Mac Nessa rose like one still heavy with a draught of poppy juice, and steadying his weight against the main roof-tree of his hall, he swore a mighty oath. 'Dead men are beyond our recall, but the heavens are above us and the earth beneath us and the sea around us; and surely unless the earth gape and swallow us and the seas roll in and engulf the land, and the heavens fall and crush us beneath their weight of stars, I will set every woman by her own hearth again and every cow in her own byre.'

Then, even as Maeve had done in Connacht, he called for the black goat to be slain and the Cran-Tara sent out through the length and breadth of Ulster from east to west, and from the northmost headlands to the borders of Murthemney. And many of his warriors he called on by name to answer the summons; those long dead as well as those yet living, for the clouds of the Great Weakness still clung about his brain.

And as the Weakness passed from all Ulster, the warriors flocked in, grimly joyful, to answer the summons. And from end to end, the province rang with the sharpening of sword and spear on weapon-stone, the buckling on of war gear and the harnessing of chariots.

In a few days all was ready, and half the host under the King himself swept from Emain Macha southward, and the other half led by Celthair Son of Uthica Hornskin came thundering from the west along the very track of Queen Maeve. And on the way the King's host fell in with a rieving band of eight score of the men of Meath, driving away in their midst many women roped together and herded like driven cattle, and they warmed their sword hands for the sterner work in store by slaying every one of the rievers and freeing the women to go back to their own hearths.

Maeve and her hosts had had word of their coming, and they were already falling back towards Connacht, for they were in no case now to meet the unscathed war host of Ulster. But when they reached Slemon Midi, the Hill of the Slain, the two halves of the Ulster host were near to outflanking them on either side, and they knew that they must stand and give battle. And Maeve with a wild and heavy heart, sent Mac Roth who had been her scout before, to view the Ulster horde on the Plain of Garach and bring her word as to its size and strength.

Mac Roth went, and from the northern slopes of Slemon Midi looked out over the Plain. He looked long and hard under his hand, and then went back, deeply troubled, to Maeve with word of what he had seen.

She was sitting beside one of the watch fires, for though the evening was a soft one for the edge of winter, suddenly she was cold to her heart's core. And Fergus Mac Roy lounged beside her on a black wolfskin rug, with his sword across his knees.

'Well, and what did you see?' demanded the Queen.

'At first when I looked out over the Plain, I saw it full of deer and other wild things, all heading south as though they would be running from a heath fire in the hot days of summer.'

'No heath fire drove *those*, but the war hosts of Ulster closing in through their forests,' said Fergus, smiling in his brown beard.

'And then presently as I watched, there came a mist flowing down the glens and leaving only the hilltops clear like islands in the white sea of it. And I could not see what lay below the mist, but out of it there came thunder and flashes as of lightning, and then a great rushing wind that all but hurled me from my feet. And since there was no more to be seen, I came back to bring you the word.'

'What is it that he tells us? Is it magic?' Maeve demanded turning to Fergus beside her.

And Fergus still smiled in his beard. 'Ach no, the mist will be the deep breathing of the war host as they march, and the lightning the flashing of their angry eyes, and the thunder will be the clangour of their weapons and their war chariots and the drumming of the horses' hooves.'

'We have warriors of our own to meet them,' said Maeve.

'And assuredly you will be needing them,' Fergus still smiled, 'for I tell you, my Queen, that in all Ireland, in all the world, there are none who can lightly face the men of Ulster in their wrath.'

And Queen Maeve rose to her feet. 'That, we will be putting to the proof,' she said.

The two war hosts came together in the Plain of Garach, below Slemon Midi; the Irish host led by Maeve herself and by Fergus Mac Roy with his great two-edged sword which was said, when swung in battle, to leave a wake of coloured light like the arc of the rainbow.

Charging three times into the heart of the enemy, he came face to face with Conor the King and rushed upon the gold-bordered shield with sword up to strike, crying, 'This for Deirdre and the Sons of Usna! This for the sons of Fergus Mac Roy!'

But Cormac Coilinglass the King's son, though he fought at Fergus's shoulder, sprang between them, crying, 'No, Fergus of the Red Branch! Remember *he is the King*!' and at the sound of the Prince's voice, Fergus swung away, and found before him instead Conall of the Victories, red with wounds, and laughing at him along his sword blade.

'Too hot!' Conall cried, 'Too hot is Fergus against his own people for a wanton woman's sake!' And Fergus rounded from him also, from all the Ulster warriors, with a groan, though indeed Deirdre had been the least of the reasons that cried in him for revenge. But his battle fury raged within him, and scarce knowing what he did, he struck with his rainbow sword among the hills; and it is said that that is why the three Maela of Meath are flat-topped as though their crests had been sliced off, to this day.

Cuchulain in his mountain fastness, heard the crash of the weapon-blows among the hills, and they troubled his darkness and splintered it apart and called him up out of it, and at last he opened his eyes, and looked frowning about him, until he found Laeg the Charioteer squatting at the foot of his bed of piled bracken. 'What is the meaning of this crashing among the hills?'

And Laeg got up and bent over him. 'The men of Ulster have roused at last from their stupor, and the battle is joined,' he said, 'and that you will be hearing is the sword play of Fergus Mac Roy.'

'Then it is time that I was rousing also,' Cuchulain said, and sprang to his feet, and he seemed to swell and grow taller, as in the onset of his battle frenzy, so that the strips of his spare cloak with which Laeg had bound his wounds burst and flew off him, and he shouted to his charioteer. 'What do you stand there gaping for? Help me with my war gear, then let you go and yoke the team!'

And so in a while the two battling war hosts alike heard the thundering of the war chariot of Cuchulain and saw it whirling towards them in the midst of its great shining cloud of dust, and cried out in triumph or despair, 'The Hound of Ulster! It is the Hound of Ulster!' And Cuchulain, yelling his war cry behind his flying team, crashed like a thunderbolt into the battle.

In the raging heart of all things he came upon Fergus Mac Roy broadside on, and yelled to him, 'Turn to me—to me, Fergus Mac Roy, and I will wash you as foam in a pool, I will go over you as the tail goes over the cat, I will smite you as a mother smites her bairn!'

'Who calls so to me?' shouted Fergus, snatching the reins from his driver and wrenching round his team.

'Do you not hear them cry my name? Cuchulain the Hound of Ulster! Now let you keep your half of the bargain we made down yonder by the ford!'

For an instant amid the swirling tumult of battle they looked at each other across the chariot rims, and then Fergus said, 'I have not forgotten my half of the bargain,' and bade his charioteer to swing the team again and bring them out of battle.

And as the word went round, under the dust storm of the fighting, the men of Leinster and the men of Munster also went after him, so that before the shadows began to lengthen, Maeve could number to her standard none but her own seven sons and the war bands of Connacht alone. Yet what were left of them fought on like heroes, like boars brought to bay.

It was high noon when Cuchulain entered the fight, and when the sunset light ran royal gold through the blackened heather, his great war chariot was but two wheels and a tangle of splintered ribs and torn oxhide, and the host of Connacht was in full flight towards Roscommon.

Cuchulain, leading one wing of the pursuit, came upon a wild woman crouching under a broken chariot with two dead horses in the yoke-harness, who cried to him with outstretched hands, 'Your mercy upon Maeve of Connacht!'

'I am not wont to kill women,' Cuchulain said, 'even Queens deserted by their host.'

'The Curse of the Morigon upon them! Upon Ailell most of all!'

'Too long you have kept that one like a hound in leash. And now that the leash is broken, what does he owe you, that he should stay to die standing over you?'

But he called up his own warriors and, no man looking at her, they mounted her into the chariot of Conall of the Victories, and closed up about her, and so got her safely to the Shannon and across it into Athlone. 'For I do not think that Connacht will lightly come cattle raiding into Ulster again for a while and a while,' Cuchulain said.

So ended the Cattle Raid of Quelgney. And after it all, the Brown Bull was never any gain to the Connacht herds, for the White Bull of Ailell knew of his coming, and broke his shackles and came thundering to fight for the lordship of the herd, and in Maeve's cattle run the two brutes fought until the earth shook and the hills shuddered and rang with their tramplings and bellowings. And the Brown Bull killed the White and kneeled on him and trampled him and tore him apart with his horns, and flung the rags of him about so that they fell from Rath Cruachan to Tara of the Kings. Then he rushed bellowing about the land until his heart burst and he fell dead, vomiting black blood, at the place which is called the Ridge of the Bull to this day.

Back at the Royal Palace of Rath Cruachan, Ailell said to Maeve—and himself speaking in a voice that he had never used to her before—'Now we will make a seven years' peace with Ulster, in my name as well as in yours.'

And Maeve, not daring to be revenged on him as she would have liked, for she knew how thin in that hour was her hold on her people, said, 'We? Are you so sure, then, that you will still be King of Connacht in seven years?'

'No man—and no woman—may be sure that he will still draw breath in seven years, yet whether I am still King of Connacht or no the empty places beside the hearths of Connacht shall call to men's minds that it was you that ordered this raid on Ulster, and if you seek to do the thing again you may find your hold upon the war host something less sure than once it was!'

14. The Coming of Connla

FOR a long time after the fight at the ford and the death of
Ferdia, for a long while after the wounds of his body were
healed, it was as though Cuchulain were wounded in his mind;
he had no joy left to him even in hunting, no joy in harp song,
nor in the touch of Emer's hands. But little by little, as the
months passed into years, that wound also healed, though
maybe the scar of it never quite ceased its aching, and he
returned to his old ways. The fire of life burned high in him
again, and he answered as of old to the call of any adventure
that came his way.

And many and many were the adventures that came, and if
they did not come, he went out to seek them. Once he even
went down into Tir-Nan-Og, the Land of Youth, to fight for
Labraid of the Quick Sword, among the Fairy Kind. That was
the time he met with Fand, who was wife to Manannan the
Lord of the Sea, and loved her from one new moon until the
next. For always he was quick to fall in love, but always he

forgot the new love in a while and a while, and came back to Emer as a man comes again to his own hearth after a day's hunting. And that time too, he came back to her, and she waiting as she had learned to wait until he chose to come, among the apple trees of Dūn Dealgan.

It was many years now since his warrior training, and Cuchulain would have forgotten Aifa of the Golden Hair as completely as the others that came after, save that, as time passed and Emer bore him no child, he would wonder now and then, when he saw the boys at hurley, whether he had a son growing up for him somewhere away beyond the Land of Shadows. And at such times Emer would know what was in his mind, and it would be to her as though a small sharp dagger were turning in her heart.

And then one summer day, when King Conor Mac Nessa and some of his lords had been racing their horses together on the hard white wave-rippled sand of the coast below Dūn Dealgan they beheld, coming in to shore, a little boat that lifted and dipped gull-wise into the troughs of the waves. It was sheathed in plates of bronze instead of dressed skins; and in it sat a boy with gilded oars in his hands, and his head shone in the sunlight and dancing water-light, more golden than the oars. There was a small pile of stones in the boat, and ever and again as the King and his nobles watched, the boy would fit a stone into his sling and cast at one of the sea birds that swooped and circled overhead, and always he cast in such a way that he did not kill the bird but brought it down alive to his feet; and then he would take it up and caress it, and cast it back none the worse into the blue air. And all kinds of other strange and fantastic things he did, showing off joyously for the watching men on the shore.

But Conor shook his head that was beginning to be grey

streaked like a badger, watching still as the boat came into the shallows, and he said, 'If the grown men of that boy's country were to come against us they would grind us as the quern stone grinds barley. Woe to any land into which that boy shall come, for when he is grown to manhood it is in my mind that no land will be large enough to hold him!' And as the keel ran up on to the white sand, he said to Cethern Son of Findtan, who stood beside him, 'Go you and bid him turn back along the sea trail by which he came.'

But when Cethern delivered the King's word, the boy only laughed and tossed up his head like a high-spirited colt, and said, 'Surely here is a poor welcome for a stranger! But I will not turn back for you.'

'It is not my word, but the King's,' Cethern said.

And the boy replied, 'Then I will not turn back for the King, nor for any man!'

So Cethern returned to the King and told him what the boy had said.

Then Conor Mac Nessa turned to Conall of the Victories. 'Go you and see if you can make my message clearer—also something sharper if need be.'

So Conall drew his leaf-shaped bronze sword and strode into the shallows, but the boy saw him coming and fitted a stone into his sling and let fly at him with a high triumphant shout; and the wind of the sling stone passing by his cheek knocked Conall down, and before he could rise again, spitting out salt water, the boy was upon him and had wrenched his arms behind his back and bound them with his own shield strap.

Then the King, more certain than ever of the danger that lay in a boy of such powers, sent another of his champions to demand where he came from, and another and another; and each as he came, the boy treated as he had treated Conall of the Victories.

When upward of a score of the Red Branch Warriors had suffered in the same way, the King spoke again urgently to Cethern Mac Findtan. 'Ride to Dūn Dealgan and bring me back Cuchulain to do battle against this boy whom even Conall of the Victories is powerless to overcome.'

So Cethern mounted his horse and rode to Dūn Dealgan a few miles off, in a smother of blown dune sand.

Cuchulain was in the women's chambers with Emer his wife when the King's summons reached him, and he would have caught up his weapons and gone at once in answer, but Emer swept up from the cushioned bench on which she had been sitting at her embroidery frame, and caught him by the arm. 'Cuchulain, let you not go!'

He looked at her, and the laughter flashed up in the sad face of him. 'Not go, when the King summons?'

'You are ill,' Emer said quickly. 'Only a while since you were complaining of pain in your head. It is in my mind that you should go to bed now, and I will send word to the King for you.'

'Emer, you say foolish things. There is no pain in my head. Why should I not go?'

'I do not know, but there is a shadow on me, and it comes from you . . . It is in my mind that the son Aifa promised you might be just such a one as this boy!'

Cuchulain reached for his sword to belt it on, and she saw that he meant to go for all that; and she clung round his neck as she had used to do in their first years together. 'Listen, my Hound, do not you go out to the King, for the fear is in me that if you do, it may be to slay your own son!'

But Cuchulain kissed her and pulled her arms away. 'Ach

now, leave be, my girl; the King sends for me to do battle with this stranger, and though it be young Connla himself, I must slay him if need be, for the honour of Ulster.'

'Honour!' cried Emer, and the eyes of her flashing battle sparks. 'Always this talk of honour with you men! It is more to you than truth, more than love; you must be for ever slaying each other and being slain; and what is it to your lordly selves, the hearts of the women you break behind you?'

'It was not so you spoke when I came wooing you under the apple trees, Emer.'

'I was a little green hard apple—I have learned somewhat since those days—I might have been the boy's mother.'

But Cuchulain scarcely heard her, for he had gone striding to the door and was calling for Laeg to yoke his chariot.

And when it was done, and the horses brought trampling round into the forecourt, he sprang in and taking the reins himself, as he often did when he did not need his hands for spear and shield, he drove out after Cethern Mac Findtan.

They followed the coast until they came to the stretch of hard white sand, and there they found the King and his hearth companions standing with their horses and looking on with a grim air of waiting, some of them cherishing wounds or the red weals of their lately loosed bonds, while the boy, seemingly as fresh as in the moment when he sprang ashore, stood at the surf's edge, tossing up his throw-spears in shining arcs and making them spin in the sunshine like whirling lesser suns, to amuse himself and pass the time.

Cuchulain sprang down from the chariot, and bidding Laeg to wait with the rest, he strolled forward alone. 'That is a pretty play that you make with your weapons, child; do they teach all the babes to play so, in the land that you come from?'

'Only to those that are not cross-eyed,' said the boy, laughing. 'For the game has its hazards,' and he sent the spear again spinning skyward, and caught it when the down-wheeling point was within a finger's breadth of Cuchulain's breast.

'That was neatly done at all events,' said Cuchulain, who had not moved. 'Tell me now, who you are and what place you come from.'

'That is a thing that I may not tell.' The boy let the spear rest quiet now, in his hand.

'No man who sets foot within the borders of Ulster and refuses to tell either his name or the place whence he comes, is likely to be living long afterwards.'

'That's as maybe,' said the boy. 'Still I may not tell.'

'Then best be making ready to die with it untold.'

'I am ready,' said the boy; and with the words scarcely spoken they sprang together in the shallows. For a while they fought with their swords, so that the sparks flew up from the blades on the sea wind, as the salt spray flew about their legs. And Cuchulain knew that he had met one whose sword-play matched his own, and his heart leapt in the fierce joy of equal combat, until the boy with a swift outward flick of the wrist, delicately shored off a lock of his dark flying hair.

Then Cuchulain laughed sharp in his throat, and flung his sword away back to the sand behind him. 'That is enough of blade-play between you and me,' and leapt upon the boy like a mountain cat. And the boy sent his own sword spinning in the same way and sprang on to a low slab of rock near by in the surf that gave surer foothold than the shifting sand; and there they grappled together, each struggling with his bare hands to throw the other, but the boy planted his feet so strongly that they sank deep into the rock—for which reason, that place was called the Strand of the Footprints ever after—

and for all his mighty strength, Cuchulain could not shift him a hair's breadth.

Long and long they fought, as when two mighty stags battle for the lordship of the herd; until at last even they began to weary, their footing grew less firm-gripped to the rock, and suddenly with a cry and a clanging of war gear and a slipping and slithering splash, they went down locked together into the foam-laced shallows. But the boy fell uppermost and his arms were still fast about Cuchulain, and his knee on Cuchulain's chest, holding him down. The Champion was near to drowning, and then, at his final gasp, with fire in his breast and the blood roaring in his ears and his eyes full of a dazzling darkness, he heard, very dimly, a shout from the shore, and something flew humming towards where they threshed about. With a supreme effort he tore one arm free, and reaching out, caught the shaft of a great spear that came like a long tailed fish cleaving the bright boil of water above him; and the instant his hand closed on it, he knew that Laeg had flung him the Gae Bolg. Struggling half over, he drew back his arm and made the death thrust. And he felt—the sick memory on him—how it tore into the boy's belly as it had done into Ferdia's by the ford, and all the shallows about them were red with blood.

'That is a thing that Skatha never trained me to,' cried the boy. 'And I am hurt—I am hurt——'

And Cuchulain slipped clear of the slight body and lifted him and laid him across the rock; and so saw on his hand the gold ring that he had given to Aifa, fifteen summers ago.

He gathered the boy in his arms and carried him out of the shallows and laid him down on the white sand before Conor and the Lords of Ulster. 'Here is Connla my son for you,' he said, grey and cold. 'There is little enough that Ulster or Ulster's honour has to fear from him now, my Lord the King.'

'Is that the King?' the boy asked faintly, for the life was still in him.

'That is Conor Mac Nessa, your kinsman, and the King,' Cuchulain said, kneeling to support him.

'If I had five years to grow to manhood among your warriors, we would conquer the world, to the very—gates of Rome and—beyond.' And he looked up into his father's face as though already from a long way away. 'But since the thing is as it is, my father, let you point out to me the famous champions that are here; for often I have thought of the Champions of the Red Branch, and I would see them before I go.'

So one after another the Red Branch Warriors came to kneel beside him and speak their names, and then the boy said, 'So: my heart is glad that I have seen great men, and it is time that I must be away,' and turned his face against his father's shoulder and cried out once, small and plaintive like a new-born child, and the life was gone from him.

The men of Ulster dug his grave in the coarse grass, under the rest-harrow and frilled yellow sea poppies of the shore, and set up his pillar stone with deep mourning.

That was the second and the last time in all his life that Cuchulain used the Gae Bolg; and the first time he slew his dearest friend with it, and the second time he slew his only son.

15. The Witch Daughters of Calatin

FROM that time forward, the shadows began to gather about the Hound of Ulster, and with them, unknown to any man, they gathered also for Ulster itself.

And this was the way of it.

Maeve of Connacht had indeed made her seven years' peace with Conor Mac Nessa, after the battle of Garach, but at the same time, in the deepest and fiercest inner chamber of her heart, she vowed the death of Cuchulain for the shame and loss that he had brought on her and on all Connacht, and for Ailell's triumphing over her. And she set to thinking how she might bring her cherished vengeance to flower.

She found the weapons to her hand soon enough, for the widow of the Clan Calatin, whom Cuchulain had slain at the ford, not long after his death, brought forth three daughters.

They were much as their sire had been, hideous, venomous as so many poison-toads, one-eyed, wicked; and seeing them one day squatting in the peat ash at their mother's feet, Maeve knew the unripe evil and the beginning of the unholy skills that were in them. And so she took them from their mother and sent them to learn the arts of magic, not only in Ireland, but in Britain and even as far afield as Babylon, which for divination and spell casting and necromancy was the very heart of the black rose.

They grew swiftly and learned swiftly, not in the way of mortal women, and in seven years they returned to Cruachan grown to their full strength and skill and power, so that even their father would have thought twice before he stood over against them in a duel of witches now. And they bided ready till Maeve should be ready to slip them like she-wolves upon Cuchulain.

Then Maeve called to her all those others who best hated Cuchulain—she had enough to choose from, for a man does not live as the Hound of Ulster lived, and make no enemies. Chief among them was Erc, the High King of Tara, whose father Cairpre Cuchulain had slain in battle long since, and that King of Munster who would have had Emer for his own; and Lugy the son of Curoi of Kerry—that same Curoi who had proved Cuchulain Champion of all Ireland. And the way of Lugy becoming his enemy, who had once been his friend, was this:

Curoi's wife had set her love on Cuchulain, the time that he came into Kerry for his testing, and though she waited patiently for more years than one, the time came when after a bitter quarrel with Curoi her lord, she sent lying word to Cuchulain of how her lord mistreated her, and begging him to come and bring her away from Curoi's Dūn, and telling him that if he hid with his men in the woods below, he should know when the time to attack the Dūn was come by the sign of the stream that came from it running white. And she made her small blue fire and cut a long black strand of her hair and made a singing magic over it before she gave it to the woman slave who was to carry her word to Cuchulain, to be sure that he would come.

So Cuchulain came with his hearth companions, and hid in the woods; and when the time came that she thought her lord was from home, Blanid milked the three white cows with red ears that were the pride of his heart, and poured their milk into the stream so that it ran white down to the woods where Cuchulain waited.

Then Cuchulain led his war band out of the woods to storm the Dūn. But Curoi had suspected something, and returned in secret, so that instead of taking it by surprise, they found warriors armed and ready and Curoi himself in their midst. The fighting was sore and long, but none the less they broke through at last and Curoi was slain and Cuchulain carried away the Queen, Blanid. He had meant to bring her back to Emain Macha, but that was not in her Fate, for Fercartna, Curoi's favourite song maker, went with them, pretending that he also was glad to be free of his lord yet in truth with the hope of avenging him; and he bided his time on the journey, until one evening he found himself near Blanid as she stood on the cliff edge of Beara looking out to sea, and he flung his arms round her and leapt with her over the cliff, so that both together they were dashed to pieces on the sea-washed rocks beneath.

And so it was that Lugy, who had been Cuchulain's friend, carried hatred in his heart towards him, and gladly answered Maeve's summons when it came.

Maeve knew that the Great Weakness of the Ulster warriors

would surely come upon them again as their need for strength grew sorer, and that once again it would be left to Cuchulain to defend the Gap of the North until they recovered. 'Only,' she said, 'this time we must have a yet greater war host than we had before,' and she sent Lugy southward to summon the King of Munster, and Erc to rouse out the chief men of Leinster to join them.

Only no one called forth old Fergus Mac Roy, for Maeve said, 'We shall never make an end of the Hound with Fergus among us,' and instead she bade the daughters of Calatin to put a spell of quietness upon him so that he remained in his Dūn, taking no heed of the world beyond his own hunting runs.

So the war host of the Four Provinces gathered to Cruachan by the Hill of the Lordly Ones, and from there they drove out against the Plains of Bregia and Quelgney.

Word came to Conor that his borders were being harried by the men of Munster and Connacht and all Ireland, but already the Great Weakness was upon him, and all too well he knew that all his warriors must be in the same case, save for Cuchulain who was in his own place at Murthemney. So he called for Levarcham, oldest of the women of Emain Macha, and said, 'Go you and bring Cuchulain here to me, for it is chiefly against himself that Maeve has again gathered the war host.'

'And how if he will not come?' grumbled the old woman. 'He has little enough care for his own skin, that one.'

'Fool! How should he come, if you are mad enough to speak to him of his own skin? Bid him to come without delay, for Conor the King would have his counsel for the saving of Ulster.'

So old Levarcham went with the King's word to Dūn Dealgan; and at first Cuchulain would not listen to her, but in the end she prevailed, and he summoned Laeg to yoke the chariot, and while he made ready his war gear, Emer called for her own chariot, and sent the women slaves and the children and the best of the cattle away into the secret glens of Slieve Cuillen where they might be safe; and then with Levarcham they set out for Emain Macha.

When they reached the King's Dūn, the women came out with the harpers and song-makers, who were not subject to the Great Weakness when it struck down the fighting men; and they welcomed them and swept them into the House of the Red Branch, and set them down to feasting and the sweet music of the harp. For Conor had said to them, 'Cuchulain I leave in your hands, to save him from the hatred of Maeve and the dark power of the Witch Daughters. See that you do not fail me, for if he goes down the strength and prosperity of Ulster go down for ever.'

Meanwhile the war hosts of Ireland had reached Murthemney, and finding Cuchulain gone from Dūn Dealgan, they wasted no time on the place, but the three Witch Daughters flew on the wind to Emain Macha, and set themselves down in the meadow below the Royal Dūn and began to pull up tufts of grass; and by their witch arts, from the grass stems and withered alder leaves and fuzz-balls, they made the semblance of mighty war hosts, so that it seemed to Cuchulain, starting up from the feast-table, that the Dūn was being attacked, and on all sides were the shouts of battling men and the smoke of burning buildings going up, so that it was all that Emer and those with her could do to hold him back. They cried out to him that it was but the magic of the Daughters of Clan Calatin, seeking to draw him out to his death. Then he looked about him like one rousing from a drugged sleep, and sat down once more, pressing his hands across his forehead. But again and again the madness leapt upon him and he sprang from his seat, drawing his sword to rush out and fight, and each time it was harder for his friends to hold him back. For three days it went on so, and Cuchulain's mind was confused and darkened by the ceaseless sounds of battle and the music of the harp of the Lordly People that mingled it through and through, so that although part of him believed old Cathbad when he told him that it was witchcraft, and he even seemed to listen when his Druid grandfather said to him, 'Only bide quiet for a few more days for it is a seven day magic and will burn itself out,' and nodded when they told him that word had gone to Conall of the Victories, who was away receiving the yearly tribute from the Islands, and being out of Ulster might have escaped the Weakness, and that in a few days Conall would have returned to his aid, yet time and again he would leap up, crying the old war cries, and struggle so fiercely to rush out against the phantom host, that the friends who thronged about him and held him back did so at the risk of their lives.

On the fourth morning, Conor roused himself and dragged his pain-wracked wits together, and sent for Cathbad and for Emer and the rest of the women of the Red Branch House, among them Lendabair, the wife of Conall of the Victories, who had some influence with Cuchulain. And he spoke to them urgently, while they stood about his skin-piled sleeping-place. 'Have you thought how you will keep Cuchulain safe among you yet another day and two more to follow?'

'Indeed we have thought and thought, and it is a thing that none of us know,' said Lendabair, and she biting her knuckles like one that is near to her wit's end.

'I will tell you, for I also have been thinking,' said Conor. 'You must take him away from here into Glean-na-Bodha, the Deaf Valley. For if all the men of Ireland were to stand about the rim of that valley, and they letting out their wildest war cries, no one in the valley would hear a sound. Bring him there, and keep him there, until the enchantment be spent and Conall of the Victories comes to be at his shoulder.'

'I cannot go with them,' Emer said, 'for with the war host of Maeve rieving through Murthemney, my place is in Dūn Dealgan, that the household be not left leaderless with none to keep the roofs on the byres. But let Lendabair be beside him in my stead; he will listen to her maybe more than to me, for he has never greatly listened to me,' and this she said, not in bitterness, but only as one speaking a true thing.

Then it was agreed, and Cathbad went to Cuchulain, and said, 'Dear son, you have been pent in this place overlong like a mewed falcon; now today I am holding a feast in my house for the harpers and song-makers and the women of the Red Branch. Let you come with us now, for you have ever loved the music of the harp, and today we will hear such harping as few men hear in their lives.'

'I am well enough where I am, and in little mood for music,' said Cuchulain, clenching his fists at the sounds of battle in the air.

'Remember that it is geise to you not to refuse a feast,' said Cathbad.

'As it was to Fergus Mac Roy, and see what came of it! My grief! What a time is this for me to be feasting and making merry, with all Ulster going up in flames, and the men of Ulster helpless under the Weakness, and the men of Ireland putting scorn and laughter on me, that I have run from them like a frightened hare!'

'What time is it for you to be breaking your geise?' said Cathbad.

And Emer put her arms about his neck and held him close.

'Hound, my Hound, I never but once tried until now to hold you back from any venture, whatever the hazard of it. So now do not refuse me this time, my first love, my darling of all the men of the world. Go with Cathbad and Lendabair.'

And Lendabair went to him and took his hands, 'Ah, come, Cuchulain, the men of Ireland shall not laugh long; only let you wait for Conall of the Victories.'

Long and long they argued with him, until at last he yielded, and took his leave of Emer, and grim and silent mounted into the chariot when Laeg brought it round to the forecourt of the Red Branch House, and went with them wherever they wished.

So they brought him into the valley of Glean-Na-Bodha. And when he realised what place it was, Cuchulain cursed and beat his fists together. 'Now of all places this is the worst that I could come to, for now indeed the men of Ireland will say that the Hound has run from them with his tail between his legs!'

'You gave your word to Lendabair,' Laeg said quickly, 'that you would not go against the men of Ireland without her leave.'

'If I did so,' said Cuchulain, 'then it is right for me to hold to my word.'

The chariots were unyoked, and the Grey of Macha and the Black Seinglend were turned loose to graze in the glen. Then they all went in to the house that Cathbad had sent his servants ahead to make ready for them. They set Cuchulain in the chief place at the High Table and began to make a great show of laughter and pleasantness all about him, just as they had done at his coming into the Red Branch Hall. While in their midst Cuchulain sat black browed and taut as an overstrung bow, listening to every sound from beyond their merriment.

He had not long to wait in his listening; for when the Witch

Daughters found him gone from the Red Branch House, they rose high into the air like an upswirl of withered leaves, and on a blast of moaning wind they whirled over the whole of Ulster, searching out every wood and valley until they came at last over Glean-Na-Bodha. And there below them, among other horses and chariots, they saw Black Seinglend and the Grey of Macha grazing, and Laeg leaning on his spear close by. And by that they knew that Cuchulain was somewhere in the valley. And as they eddied downward they saw the timber hall under the eaves of the woods, and heard the laughter and the sound of harp song coming from within.

They took thistle stalks and little fuzz-balls and withered leaves as before, and made of them the appearance of vast war hosts, so that it seemed that all the world beyond the valley was full of swiftly moving men, and everywhere were wild yells and chatterings, the cries of wounded men and the wailing of women and the neighing of horses, and demon laughter and the braying of war horns; and everywhere it seemed was fire and smoke as though all Ulster were burning.

Within Cathbad's feast-hall they heard the dreadful uproar, and men and women began to shout their laughter and to sing to the harp and clap their hands and do all that they could think of to keep the magic outcry from reaching Cuchulain's ears. But the tumult was beyond drowning, and Cuchulain sprang up, crying that he heard the men of Ireland despoiling the whole province.

But Cathbad rose towering over him and caught him by the shoulders and said, 'Let it pass by. It is only the tumult made by the Witch Daughters, to draw you out of the safety of this place, that they may make an end of you.'

And Cuchulain turned away and dashed his hand against the roof-tree of the hall so that his knuckles bled. And then he sat down again and held his head in his hands. And the Daughters of Calatin went on for a while and a while, making all the air of the glen to throb with the wild shrieks of their phantom war host. But they understood at last that Cathbad and the woman and the song-makers all together were too strong for them. And then at last Bave, the most hideous of the three, went down to the very door of the feast-hall, and there she put on the likeness of one of Lendabair's women who had not accompanied her, and she beckoned Lendabair out to speak with her.

Lendabair went out to her, thinking that she must have brought some word from Emain Macha, and Bave, finger on lip, bade her and the other women who had come with her to follow where she led. Then she took them a long way down the glen, drawing them on by telling them always that it was a little farther and a little farther, until she judged that they were far enough from the hall; and then she raised a thick mist about them and put on them a spell of straying that would keep them from finding their way back until it was too late; and left them wandering.

Then she made a spell to make herself like Conall's wife and she flew back to the feast-hall and through the door and flung herself at Cuchulain's knees, her eyes haggard and her bright hair wild, crying out to him, 'Up and out, Cuchulain! Dūn Dealgan is burning and Murthemney destroyed, and all Ulster trampled down by the men of Ireland! And all men will say that it lies at my door, for I held you back! Go now, swiftly, swiftly! Or Conor will be my death!'

'Truly it is hard to trust in women,' Cuchulain said, 'for it was indeed yourself said that you would not give me leave for all the riches in the world!' But he sprang up even as he spoke, and flung on his cloak and strode out, shouting to Laeg to yoke the horses and make ready the chariot. And though Cathbad and the remaining women followed him out, striving by every means in their power to hold him back, they might as well have sought to hold marsh fire or mountain mist between their fingers, for the air was still full of the tumult of battle, and he seemed to see the whole war host of Ireland trampling through Ulster, the roofs of Emain Macha and Dūn Dealgan in a great smoke lit with bursts of red flame, and the corpse of Emer tossed out over Dūn Dealgan ramparts.

Laeg went to do his bidding as slowly as might be, he who had never been heavy-hearted in that task before; and when he shook the bridles towards the horses as he always did to summon them, they started away from him, snorting and tossing their heads and flying round in wary circles, show-ing the whites of their eyes. And the Grey of Macha in particular would not let him come within halter's length. 'Truly this is an omen of ill things to come,' said Laeg to him-self, and he groaned, and went to Cuchulain. 'If you would have the Grey of Macha into the yoke this day, you must do the thing yourself. I have never known him unwilling until now, but I swear by the Gods my people swear by, that I cannot so much as set hand on him!'

So Cuchulain strode out with the bridles; but the Grey shied away from him as from Laeg. 'Brother,' Cuchulain cried, 'you have never behaved so ill to me before. If you love me, come, for we must go out against the enemies of Ulster, you and I.'

Then the Grey of Macha came at last, his head hanging; and standing there to accept the bridle he let great heavy tears of blood fall on Cuchulain's feet.

16. The Death of Cuchulain

So at last the chariot was yoked, despite all that the others could say or do, and like a man bound in an evil dream, Cuchulain set out for Murthemney. And all the while he cursed and raved at Laeg for more speed, until they drove like a thundercloud before a gale of wind, and the trees and bushes and grasses bent back and streamed out at their passing, as before a great storm rushing by. And ever in Cuchulain's ears was the tumult of battle, and ever before his eyes the fire and the demon war hosts and the broken body of Emer tossed out over the ramparts of her own Dūn.

Yet when he came to Dūn Dealgan among its apple trees, it was just as it had always been, and Emer came out to him with her pleated crimson mantle about her and the gold ornaments hung in her hair. And she set her hands on the chariot bow, and said, 'Welcome home, my lord. Let you come down from your chariot now, for the evening meal is waiting.'

'It must wait on,' Cuchulain said. 'I go against the war hosts of the Four Provinces—I have seen them gathering—I have seen the smoke of their fires even on the walls of Emain Macha.'

'That was but the enchantments of the Witch Daughters of Calatin. Give them no heed, and in two more days they will be gone, and Conall of the Victories will be here to drive his war team into battle beside yours.'

'I cannot wait for Conall of the Victories! I tell you, woman, I see them, I hear them even now—there is not one heart-beat of time to be lost!'

And Emer saw that there was no holding him, for the bonds of witchcraft had him by the soul. 'At least you can wait while I bring you a cup of wine to slake the way-dust in your throat,' she said, and while he waited, fretting and starting like the horses at the yoke pole, she ran and fetched Greek wine in a cup of age-darkened amber. But when she held it up to him and he stooped to take it, he started back with a cry, for between her hand and his, the cup was brimming with blood.

'My grief! It is not wonderful that others forsake me when my own wife offers me a drink of blood!'

Then she snatched the cup from him and flung out the blood and filled it again with wine; but that time also, and yet a third time, the wine in the cup turned to blood as he stooped to take it. And the third time he flung the cup against the pillar stone of the house, so that the amber broke into shards like great golden petals and the blood splashed all down the pillar stone. 'The fault is not yours; my Fate has turned against me and now I know indeed that this time I shall not come home to you from battle. Ach well, I took the Fate on me with my eyes open, on the day that I chose to take the weapons of manhood. I have known how it would be.'

'Wait!' Emer begged, her hands gripping the sides of the chariot. 'Only wait, and your Fate will turn again!'

'Not for all the power and the golden riches in the world!' Cuchulain said, 'nor for anything you can say, Emer, Falcon-of-my-Heart. Never since the day that he received his weapons has the Hound of Ulster hung back when the war horns sounded, and he'll not change the way of it now, for they do say that a great name outlasts life.'

And he stooped and kissed her once, so that her lips were bruised, and struck her hands from the chariot rim, and cried to Laeg, 'Drive on, my brother, for we have lingered too long by the way!'

And the horses sprang forward from the goad and the dust cloud rose between him and Emer, and they drove on south like a storm cloud before the gale.

Presently they came to the river ford, and kneeling beside the shallows was a girl with skin as white as curds and hair that hung about her yellow as broom flowers; and she was washing a pile of bloodstained garments, and keening to herself as she washed, as the women keen for their dead, and as she lifted a crimsoned tunic from the water, Cuchulain saw that it was his own.

'Do you not see? Will you not heed this last warning and go back?' Laeg said.

'Whether or not I turn back, it will be all one, for my Fate is on me,' said Cuchulain, and his voice and his eyes were his own again, as though the madness had left him. 'And what is it to me that the woman of the Lordly Ones washes bloody clouts for me? There shall be others than myself lying in their blood ere I have finished my game of spears with the warriors of Ireland.' And he looked round at his charioteer. 'But let you turn aside if you have a mind to, for the call is not for you. Go back to Emer and tell her how sore my heart is to leave her, after the many times that I have come back to her in gladness out of strange places and far countries.'

'She knows without telling of mine,' Laeg said. 'Your Fate has been mine too long to change the way of it now,' and he steadied the horses down to the water, and as they crossed, the maiden flickered out as a marsh-light flickers out; and where she had been was nothing but an alder tree trailing its hair in the water.

Later they turned on to the track from Meadhon to Luachair. And beside the track they came upon three hideous ancient women, each blind of the left eye, and the horses shied across the track at sight of them. They had made a fire of sticks and were roasting the carcass of a dog over it on spits of rowan wood; and Cuchulain would have passed them by, for he knew well enough that it was not for his good that they were there. But one of them called to him, 'Stay awhile, Cuchulain, and eat with us.'

'I will not then, for I have no time for eating just now,' Cuchulain called back.

'If we had a great feast to offer, you would stay. It does not become the great and powerful to despise the small and humble folk!'

Then Cuchulain, for the sake of courtesy, bade Laeg to draw rein, and stepped down from the chariot, and took the shoulder of the dog from one of the old women and ate it, well though he knew that his geise forbade him to eat the flesh of a hound because of the hound of Cullen who had given him his name; for he thought, 'It is all one. My Fate is on me no matter what I do or do not do.' But he took care to take the meat with the left hand, and as he did so, that hand was stricken so that the goodness went out of it.

Then he sprang back into the chariot and bade Laeg drive on—on—on, and they thundered on down the track of Meadhon-Luachair that passes hard beneath Slieve Fuad through the Gap of the North. And it was in his mind how he had driven that way seven years before.

Now Erc Son of Cairbre had driven ahead with the scouting chariots along the wooded skirts of Slieve Fuad, and saw him coming in a great cloud of dust that was shot through with red gold like a dust cloud at sunset by the Hero light that played about his head; his spear crimson-bladed in his hand, and the great black Crow of Battles flapping above him. 'Cuchulain is upon us!' he shouted to the men about him, and wheeled his horse and was away back to the war host coming up behind. 'Cuchulain comes in a cloud of fire! The magic has drawn him forth at last, but he comes like no spellbound victim to the knife! So now let us be ready to receive him worthily!'

So they formed their foot warriors into a shield-hedge with their lime-washed bucklers, and raised the war shout; and the heads of their spears were as the leaves of a summer forest, and on either side and behind the gaps in the foot ranks the chariots were ranged.

And when Cuchulain saw the hosts of Ireland standing waiting like a weaponed forest all across the plain of Murthemney, from Slieve Fuad into the foot-slopes of Slieve Cuillen, he cried to Laeg to make the pace yet swifter; and as they drove furiously down upon them, he plied the Champion's Thunder Feat against them until their dead were scattered thick and far as sands on the shore, as hailstones when a thunderstorm has passed, as buttercups in a summer meadow.

Then one of the bards who were with the war host sprang into the horses' track, crying, 'Cuchulain, Hound of Ulster, your spear to me!' For the three Witch Daughters had foretold that Cuchulain's great throw-spear should be the death of three kings that day, and no kings were there save those of Munster and Leinster and Connacht.

Among all men it was a point of honour to refuse nothing that a bard might demand. 'Yet I have greater need of it myself than you can have, this day,' Cuchulain shouted back.

'I will put a bad name on you if you refuse me, and it shall last for ever on all men's tongues.'

'There was never a bad name put on me yet, for the refusing of a gift,' Cuchulain cried. 'Take it, then, oh Song-Maker of Lugy's court!' and he flung the great spear at him with such force that it passed clear through him and killed nine men beyond.

Then Lugy himself stooped and caught up the spear and hurled it back at Cuchulain. But the horses were plunging, and instead it caught Laeg the King of Charioteers, so that he fell back with a great wound under his breast-bone. 'I am hard hit,' Laeg said. 'And what will you do for a charioteer, Cuchulain, my dear lord?'

'I will be my own charioteer,' Cuchulain said, crouching over him to draw out the spear; and Laeg helped him with his own hand, and on the bright wave of blood that came with it, the life broke out from him; and Cuchulain kissed him and laid him down on the chariot floor. Then he bound the reins round his own waist that he might have his hands free, and rushed on through the war host of Ireland.

And as he hurled along, another bard called to Cuchulain for his spear.

'There is but my spear against the Four Provinces of Ireland,' Cuchulain cried. 'I have sorer need of it than you, this day!'

'Have you forgotten that once a great king tore out his own eye because his bard asked it of him? I will put a name of reproach on all Ulster for your refusal!'

'Ulster was never yet put to shame for me.' And Cuchulain threw the great spear at the man with such strength that it passed through his head and through the heads of nine men behind him, and Cuchulain thundered on as before.

Then it was Erc Son of Cairbre Niafer, who caught up the reeking spear and hurled it back, but his aim was wilder even than Lugy's, and ploughed deep into the flank of the Grey of Macha, the King of all the Horses of Ireland, dealing him a wound that must be his death before many days were out.

Cuchulain outed his dagger and slashed the reins from his waist, and sprang forward upon the yoke pole to draw out the spear and cut through the trace that held the Grey to the chariot.

'The Gods be kind to you, my brother. May there be many mares in the plains of Tir-Nan-Og,' he said, and the great horse wheeled and plunged off through the battle, away and away leaving his blood trail behind him, to cool his mortal hurts in the Grey Lough under Slieve Fuad.

Then with the Black Seinglend dragging the chariot askew like a wounded bird, Cuchulain plunged on once more through the war host. And a third time one of the royal bards cried out to him for his spear.

'My honour does not bid me to bestow more than one gift in one day, and I have already given two,' returned Cuchulain.

'I will put a bad name upon you if you refuse me!'

'I have paid the ransom for my name,' Cuchulain said.

'Then I will call down reproach upon all Ulster!'

'I have paid my due for the honour of Ulster.'

'Then I will call it down upon your kindred and all you love!'

And at that, Cuchulain cried out, thinking of Emer, and of the dark hard King and ancient gentle Cathbad, and of Conall of the Victories even now thundering to his aid. 'That is another matter. No man should leave shame behind him with those he loves. Take the gift in kindness, then,' and he flung the great spear with such force that it passed through the bard's rib-cage and slew nine men behind him.

'You do your kindnesses ungently, Hound of Ulster,' said the bard as he fell.

Then Lugy got the spear again, and hurled it back, and it struck its third king; it struck Cuchulain who was King of all the Heroes of Ireland, full in the lower part of the breast, so that he knew he had got his death wound even as his bowels fell out from him upon the cushions of the chariot. And in the same instant the Black Seinglend reared up and swung half round on his haunches; the chariot heeled over with a splintering crash and the breaststrap broke. And the great midnight-coloured horse, maddened by the tumult and the smell of blood behind him and the splintered chariot at his heels, broke away with half the harness hanging about his neck, and galloped neighing and savaging as he went, through the heart of the enemy war host. And behind him his lord was left asprawl in the ruins of the chariot.

Then as the kings and chieftains crowded about him, Cuchulain forced himself up to his knees, and his voice came harsh in his throat and the darkness made webs before his eyes. 'I am in your hands now; give me leave to go down to the lough-side yonder for the wish is on me to drink.'

And the kings and princes looked at each other; and at last Erc Mac Cairbre said, 'So be it, then. Go down to the lough shore and drink your fill, but return into our hands afterwards.'

Cuchulain laughed, and never was there laughter with less of mirth in it. 'If I come not back, you will know where I am. I give you leave to come down and fetch what is left of me.'

Then he gathered his bowels into his breast and bound his cloak tightly about himself; and gathering the little strength

that was left in him, he staggered to his feet and went down to the lough side. And there among the whispering brown-flowered rushes he drank and washed himself, and then turned back again to die. He had not strength left to drag himself back to his enemies, but he knew that they would come after him soon enough.

There was a tall pillar stone beside the lough, and he got to it, and slung his girdle over it and knotted it about his breast, that he might meet death in his standing up and not in his lying down. And his blood ran down into the lough, and an otter came up through the shallows and lapped it.

Then the war hosts of the enemy came and gathered round, all along the shores of the lough, but none of them dared go near him for the Hero light was still on his forehead, and by that they knew that there was still a spark of life in him.

Then the Grey of Macha came back at a wounded gallop to defend his lord so long as the life lingered in him, and the Grey made three charges against the men of Ireland, and he killed fifty men with his teeth that sunset time, and thirty with each hoof, so that there is a saying yet: 'It is not sharper work than this, was done by the Grey of Macha, the time of Cuchulain's dying.'

Then a great black gore-crow flapped down and settled upon Cuchulain's shoulder, and by that they knew that he was dead. And Lugy Son of Curoi came and lifted Cuchulain's long dark hair sideways from his neck and struck off his head, while all the men of Ireland shouted in heavy triumph. Now Cuchulain's naked sword fell from his hand, and in its falling, lopped off Lugy's right hand, so that his yell mingled with the war host's shouting. They hacked off Cuchulain's right hand in satisfaction, while the Hero light faded from about his severed head, leaving it pale as the ashes of a long-dead fire.

Then all the warriors of Ireland called on Maeve to bring away the head with her to Cruachan, since it was she that had gathered the war host and made her use of the Daughters of Clan Calatin. But Maeve drew back the hem of her mantle from the blood, she who had never minded blood before, and looked down at the head with dreadful eyes. 'I will not bring it to Cruachan, I will not have it near me! Lugy struck it off, and paid for it with a hand. Let him carry it away with him!'

And so Lugy and his men set off that same night, heading for the Lifé River, and they carried Cuchulain's head and his sword hand with them.

17. The Vengeance
of Conall the Victorious

BY now the men of Ulster were all but healed of the Great
Weakness, for this time it had fallen less heavily than usual,
and maybe the magic of the Witch Daughters abroad in the
land had fought with the older spell and thinned its power.
And the Ulster war host was already gathering to fly at the
throat of its enemies. And Conall of the Victories was out
ahead of them, when he met the Grey of Macha with the life-
blood dripping from his flank.

Then Conall knew that his foster brother was dead, for the
horse would never have left him else; and he swore to keep the
promise that they had made each other as boys, that if either
were killed before the other, the one left would avenge him.
But first he must find Cuchulain's body. That was not hard to
do, for the Grey of Macha, now that he had found Conall,
had no thought but to get him back to his lord. And even had
that not been the way of it, there was the blood trail to follow,
as easily as a paved road.

So they pressed on together, the Grey galloping beside

Conall's Dewy Red, until at last they came to the lough shore below Slieve Fuad, and saw Cuchulain's headless body still bound to the pillar stone. Then the Grey of Macha went and laid his head on Cuchulain's breast.

And reining in the chariot team, Conall saw the hand of Lugy, Curoi's son, lying on the grass by Cuchulain's feet, and knew it by the thumb ring on it.

'There is another whose journey is finished,' said Conall to his own heart, 'and I know whose hand struck the last blow.' And looking again towards where the great silver horse stood with his head on his lord's still breast, he said, 'They will do well enough together until I come again,' and he wheeled the chariot and pricked the team from a stand to a gallop, and thundered away on the track of the Munster men (for the tracks of the separate war hosts left the camp by separate ways) until he came to the river Lifé; and on the way he met one of the herdsmen of Dūn Dealgan among the hills, and bade him go back and tell his mistress what had befallen.

Now Lugy could not bear to travel so fast as his war bands, by reason of his hurt and the fever that rose from it, and so he had bidden them push on while he followed more easily. And so he was no farther than the crossing of the Lifé, and was indeed just going down to bathe in the coolness of the running water.

'Keep a keen look-out across country, lest any man should come upon us unawares,' he had said.

And now the charioteer, leaning against the trunk of an alder tree to keep his watch, cried out, 'There is a man coming across the plain, and a great hurry he is in; and you would think that all the ravens in Ireland were flying over his head, and flakes of snow whitening the ground before him.'

Then Lugy scrambled quickly up the bank and looked where

he pointed; and a groan burst from him. 'That is Conall of the Victories, and the ravens that fly about his head are the sods that fly from the horses' hooves, and the snow flecking the ground before him is the froth that the horses scatter from their muzzles. Let them pass on the trail of the war host, if that may be, for I have no mind to fight him.' So they drew back clear of the ford, into the shadows of the alder break.

But when Conall was scarcely half across the ford he saw them, and bringing his horses splashing through to the farther shore, turned aside into the alder brake and reined in beside them. 'Welcome is the sight of a debtor's face, so they say.'

'In what would I be your debtor?' Lugy demanded.

'In that you slew Cuchulain my comrade and foster brother.'

'And what will clear the debt?'

'Blood will clear the debt,' said Conall of the Victories.

'If we are to fight,' said Lugy, when both had been silent for a while and a while, 'then I claim an equal combat—that you and I should fight with each but one hand.'

'That is fair enough,' said Conall, and springing down from the chariot he pulled off his girdle and turned to Lugy's charioteer. 'Let you bind my right hand behind me. See that the knots are secure.'

Then he took his sword in his left hand, and Lugy did the same, and there on the bank they fought the hardest fight that was in them, for a full half day. But when it was past noon and still Conall had gained no advantage over the other, his horse the Dewy Red who stood near by, sprang forward dragging the chariot behind him, and tore a great piece out of Lugy's side.

'Grief upon me!' cried Lugy. 'That was not in the bargain!'

'I took up the bargain for myself, to fight fair; who can bargain with a dumb beast that knows only faith to its master?'

and Conall sprang forward as he spoke, and ran his sword into Lugy's neck, and made an end.

Then leaving the charioteer to gather up his lord's body, he himself took Cuchulain's head and strong thin sword hand that he found bundled in a silken tunic in Lugy's chariot, and turned his way back to the pillar stone under Slieve Fuad.

By that time the herdsman had returned to Dūn Dealgan, and Emer knew that her lord was slain. And she called out the teams from the stables and the chariots from the chariot shed and gathered her women about her, and said, 'We must go out to the place where my lord is, and we must bring him home.'

So when Conall came back to the place of the pillar stone in the grey of dawn, he found that they were before him and had unbound Cuchulain's headless body and laid it down close by the body of the Grey of Macha, all among the slain, and all the women of Dūn Dealgan were gathered about it on the lough shore keening for their dead, with their cloaks laid across their faces.

Conall laid Cuchulain's head with his body and his sword hand to its wrist, and standing there added his own lament to the keening of the women. 'Never fell a better hero nor a stronger champion than has fallen here by the sword of Lugy Mac Curoi. Sore are our hearts for the loss of you, my brother. Cuchulain, my Hound of Ulster. Sorrow and grief it is to me that I was not beside you in the last fight; sorrow and grief that we did not go together on the Long Journey. My heart is broken in two halves for my brother, and there will be laughter no more in Ulster.'

'Let us take him home and bury him now,' said Emer.

But Conall said heavily, 'Not yet, not until I have avenged him on the men of Ireland! Bear him home if you will, but before Cuchulain lies in his grave I swear that there shall not be one tribe left unscathed nor their blood unspilled, and the whole world shall hear of the vengeance of Conall of the Victories for his brother, the Hound of Ulster!'

Then rage and madness sprang upon Conall as though it were something of Cuchulain's battle frenzy, and he leapt back into the chariot to follow the whole war host of Ireland as he had followed Lugy to his death.

The folk of Dūn Dealgan bore Cuchulain's body back to his own hall, and Emer washed the blood from it, keening over it, crying as she had been too proud ever to cry while he lived.

'Ochone! Ochone! It is many the kings and princes of the world would be keening if they knew the way it is with the Hound of Ulster now! Beautiful was this head, though it is not beautiful now, and dear to me! Dear was the strength and courage and the gentleness of your hands. Happy, happy are they that will not hear the cuckoo again, now that Cuchulain is gone. I am carried away like a branch on a dark stream; I will not bind up my hair today nor any other day. Oh my love, my love, we have been happy in our time, for if the world would be searched from the rising to the setting of the sun, the like would never be found again together in one place, of the Black Seinglend and the Grey of Macha, and Laeg and Emer and Cuchulain!'

By and by Conall came back from making his red rout through the war host of Ireland; and this time his own war bands were with him, and many more besides; and he brought many heads behind him, piled high in the chariots, that he tumbled out on the green meadow before Dūn Dealgan. The head of Erc Son of Cairbre of the Swift Horses, and the heads of the sons of Maeve, and the head of the High King of

Leinster of the speckled spears, and the three heads, evil and hideous, of the three Witch Daughters of Calatin, and many and many more.

Then Emer came out to him, wearing her most stately gown, and with the gold ornaments that Cuchulain had given her on her arms and neck. And she said, 'Welcome to you, Connall of the Victories, for you have avenged the treachery done to Ulster and to my lord. And now all that is left for you is to make a grave for my Hound—but, oh Conall, make it deep and broad enough for two, for my life is too heavy for me without the Hound.'

And Conall set his men to do as she bid, speaking no word to make her change her purpose, for he knew that it would be of no avail.

And when the grave was made to her satisfaction, Emer laid herself down beside Cuchulain among the late harebells in the grass, and said as though to him alone, 'Love of my life, my friend, my sweetheart, my own choice of all the men of the world, many is the woman envied me until today, and I was proud that they envied me, because I was yours. Still I am yours, my Hound, and now there is no wish on me to live after you.' And she set her mouth to his mouth, and gave one long sigh, and with the sigh, her life went out of her.

So Conall laid them in the same grave, and raised one pillar stone over them, and carved their names upon it in the Ogham script. And all Ulster wept for their loss: because of the story of Cuchulain the Hound of Ulster, there was no more. No more.